FEAST OF THE FALLEN

Ravenous Spirits Series

BOOK 2

RON RIPLEY

EDITED BY ANNE LAO
AND DAWN KLEMISH

ISBN: 979-8-89476-316-3
Copyright © 2025 by ScareStreet.com

Enter the Realm of Terror...

We'd like to take a moment to thank you for your support and invite you to join our VIP newsletter.

Dive deeper into the darkness with exclusive offers, early access to new releases, and bone-chilling deals when you sign up at www.ScareStreet.com.

Let the nightmares begin…

See you in the shadows,
Scare Street

PROLOGUE

Simon Mackenzie stared at the small pile of bones. Ribs, he thought. A bit of spine. Probably some unfortunate soul who crashed upon the rocks and never made it off the island again.

Mackenzie had not seen the island on any of the charts he had consulted. The North West Company offered some limited help in establishing an outpost in the area, but he wanted to make more of a name for himself. He was already a shareholder; now, he was hoping to make inroads in the trade between the Commonwealth of Massachusetts and Acadia.

He and his men had done a brisk trade in New Scotland, but the territories farther south were ripe with opportunity. The fur trade was at its zenith, and more men were coming from France and England. Even the Portuguese and the Spanish were coming more frequently, and that made what had once been a much easier job more difficult.

The company was new, but it was formidable. Their goal, maybe not publicly stated, was to take on the Hudson's Bay Company. For most traders, that meant cutting right into HBC territory. They forged west, all the way to the Pacific Northwest in some cases. But Mackenzie had other ideas. He had found the island, some twenty-five miles off the coast in inhospitable and frigid waters, and it would serve as an outpost, an advantage no one else had. The East Coast was still a land of prosperity and abundance. And he would make his mark.

Most others thought he was foolish for not venturing into the unknown territories of the West. He had thought it a good idea once, but there was more to Mackenzie's goals than discovering wealth. He wanted power. He wanted to exercise that power and show that he could be a dominant force in a land that was becoming saturated with big names, big ideas, and too much competition.

To Mackenzie, that was the mark of success. Any man could head west, discover lands untouched by civilization, and claim success. Where was the challenge? Overcoming nature was an admirable goal, but the true challenge, Mackenzie thought, was being the best among others. Overcoming the competition and coming out on top. Not just being the best alone.

Uncharted though the island might have been, it was obvious someone had been there. He thought the bones looked old. Carruthers confirmed as much, inspecting the spinal section and declaring that the body had been there for at least a decade, maybe longer.

They had landed on the western shore of the island. To the north and around the east, the rocks rose into large, impossible cliffs. But the west offered a small beach, and a small inlet into which they could bring in the boat and venture forth to see what the land offered. Unfortunately, the rocks played havoc with their hull and tore it asunder before they realized they had ventured too close. What had been planned as a simple landing had become a wreck. They fled to the shore out of necessity and would need to harvest wood and supplies to repair the hull before they could leave.

From the sea, Mackenzie saw vast swaths of forest. That meant, if nothing else, timber for building. There would likely be animals for hunting, as well. And certainly good fishing, for the waters were abundant with cod and sturgeon.

He captained a crew of a dozen men. Carruthers, the ship's medic, was the newest member and the least experienced in exploring. He had joined the expedition in the hopes of heading west, but he was amenable to Mackenzie's plans to stay on the eastern shores of the United States. Carson, Bundy, Lowell, and Ashley were also new additions from Acadia.

They were green but hungry, and they seemed like good and loyal men. Mackenzie had high hopes for success.

"Gentlemen," Mackenzie said to his assorted crew. "Let us explore. Mr. Lucas will oversee the repair work."

They had been on shore no more than five minutes when Carson discovered the bones. Some of the men were not convinced they were human at first, but Carruthers confirmed that they were.

"It's an ill omen," Lowell said, and Mackenzie waved away the idea.

"I don't believe in omens, Mr. Lowell. A man must make his own luck. Nature, chance, random happenstance? These things do not matter."

"As you say, Captain," Lowell said.

There was a steep hill to scale. The path was marred by roots and shrubs, stray rocks, and slippery footing. Carson led the way, being careful to point out the most treacherous spots, and clearing what he could to allow the other men to follow.

The island unfolded before them at the top of the hill. Forest as far as the eye could see. Nearly every tree was a maple, tall and proud and densely growing together.

"There's a path." Carson indicated a very narrow foot trail through the trees.

"Game or men?" someone asked.

"Men," Carson answered. "But old."

If men were on the island, Mackenzie could not use it. They needed to make sure it was free and unclaimed. Then he could claim it as his own for the North West Company, set up an outpost, and have an advantage in trading between the Commonwealth and Acadia. It would be a place where they could rally, rest, and plan expeditions that would cut travel time significantly while opening more opportunities. They would just need to map the passage safely to avoid the rocks. It would offer strategic advantage and safety.

The group traveled inland. Carson had his rifle at the ready, and some of the other men had pistols drawn. No one was sure to whom the island belonged, so there was safety in being cautious. Violence among traders had become more common. Disagreements led to brawls, and sometimes even deaths. So far from any shore, towns, or laws, a simple trespassing claim could easily be solved with a bullet to the head. Mackenzie kept his men ready.

The path they followed was extremely narrow and vanished entirely in places that were covered over by wild grass, and once, a patch of wild blueberries. Carson always picked it up again, and soon, they were in a clearing in the forest. Stretched out before them in a natural depression that looked almost like a bowl was a tiny settlement. Just six cabins, built from stones that must have been harvested from the shore. They sat in an open field of grass and small shrubs, with a single stream that fed into a pool near the northeastern end.

From the outside edge of the bowl, everything looked overgrown. The grass was nearly up to the doors of the little stone cabins. Whoever had built them no longer seemed to be there.

The investigation of the village proved Mackenzie correct. The houses were abandoned. Some contained relics of the former owners. There were beds, knives, tables, chairs, and bowls. It looked as though whoever lived there abandoned the place in a hurry and left their possessions behind, but it also looked as if it happened years ago.

The efforts to gather supplies to repair the ship had only just gotten underway when dark clouds from the east rolled in over the island. The wind came in cold, and hail fell with it. Mackenzie called a stop to the efforts, and the men split up among the cabins.

Despite the storm and their inability to keep working, the men were happy to have so much extra space to themselves. Two men to a cabin was a luxury compared to their accommodations on the ship. There was wood for fires, and with the supplies they brought from the ship, they cooked meals and got some rest.

The storm raged outside, and the wind howled with an eerie, menacing quality. At first, Mackenzie thought there were people outside, the men playing a joke, or perhaps someone in horrible pain. When he checked, there was nothing but the freezing wind.

The rain and hail turned to sleet. It made no sense that such a cold storm should have come in. It was still early autumn, the day had been warm, and the seas had been mild. But this was shaping up to be a winter storm, with the temperature quickly dropping enough to kill anyone who could not find shelter.

It was snowing heavily by nightfall. There was a buildup on the ground several inches deep. Mackenzie feared he and the men did not have enough firewood to make it through the night. The sudden drop in temperature was as brutal as it was unexpected.

Dawn came, and the storm still raged. Bundy came to Mackenzie to report that the food had been taken from his cabin. Carruthers was next, and Lowell after that. All the food had gone missing in the middle of the night. They had taken the supplies with them from the ship; nothing was left behind.

Mackenzie checked the crate of supplies that he had brought into his cabin. It had been emptied as well. Someone had dared to break into the captain's cabin in the middle of the night and take the food. No one knew who did it. There were no tracks in the snow.

Some of the men went into the woods to hunt. The weather meant repairing the boat was impossible, so they needed to hunker down and wait out the blizzard. Hours passed, and the men who had ventured into the woods did not return.

No one had brought clothing suitable for long-term exploration in freezing temperatures. Mackenzie began to fear the worst.

The men who remained behind began to blame each other for the missing food. With no tracks in the snow, they determined it could not have been outsiders. It had to be one of them. Mackenzie was inclined to agree, but he could not rightly say who was responsible. He did not want to believe any of his men—men he trusted—would steal food from their fellow crewmembers, but someone had done just that.

The men never returned from the hunt, and the storm continued into the second day. A search party went out after the hunters. Three more men. Gone. Five total. Those who remained grew more paranoid. They feared they were not alone on the island. The bones they had seen were an omen, just as Lowell had said. They were all doomed to die.

Mackenzie awoke to the unmistakable smell of roasting chicken on the third day. He followed it out into the storm and unrelenting snow that had built up higher and higher around the stone cabins. He'd never seen anything like it, but at that moment, he didn't care. He smelled meat cooking and followed it, freezing, and trudging through the snow to the farthest cabin from his own, pounding on the door until Carruthers opened it.

"There's no meat here, Captain," Carruthers assured him. "We're starving just like everyone else."

Mackenzie searched and found no trace of it, but the smell lingered. He thought for a moment that he saw grease on Carruthers' fingers. He said nothing as he left. His men were lying. They had turned on him, stolen from him, and put his life in jeopardy. It could not stand.

Everyone stayed in their cabins for the rest of the day.

Bundy and Morris were gone the next day, and their cabin was empty. Their tracks led into the woods. No one would volunteer to find them. Only five men remained, including Mackenzie.

Hunger pains became a distraction, but Mackenzie had survived without food before. The snow still raged the next morning. It was hard to get the cabin door open. Carruthers was missing, and so was Lowell. Only Carson and Wellesley remained. None of the missing men had taken their possessions with them. Their clothes and all of their gear remained behind.

The snow stopped on the final day. Mackenzie was alone when he woke. Carson and Wellesley were gone. Their tracks led into the forest. Both men had gone barefoot, and all their clothing was left behind.

Mackenzie took a rifle and a pistol. He headed into the forest, charging through the snow, fighting against the cold that seeped into his bones. The tracks were easy to follow. They wound through the maple trees, deeper and deeper into the forest where at least the tree cover had stopped some of the savagery of the weather and the snow was not so deep.

He walked for what must have been an hour until he came upon a clearing in the forest. A ring of seven stones sat in the middle. Though they were covered in snow, the entire ring was brilliant red. Blood saturated everything. It clung to the trunks of the nearby trees, covered the stones, and soaked into the snow, all from the pile of mutilated bodies in the center of the clearing.

The bodies of his men.

Mackenzie stared in horror. He could think of no animal that would savage men in such a fashion. Their flesh had not just been torn; it had been cut away. Chunks taken away as though they were pigs at a butcher shop. Meat had been scraped to the bone across their bodies.

He saw Carson's body, the last one on the pile. Clear, deep teeth marks were sunk into the man's face. Not the teeth of a beast; no animal of the forest did this. The teeth of a man. Someone had eaten his men. Someone had killed them for their flesh.

As Mackenzie backed away, something moved in the pile. He thought at first that one of the men had somehow endured the horrible injuries and was still living. But he was wrong.

The thing that crawled out of the pile was not one of his men. Nor was it living. Like them, it was missing flesh. It was covered in ragged, bloody meat clinging to exposed bone. A second creature climbed from the pile, and then a third. By the time Mackenzie saw the fourth, he turned and ran.

The snow slowed him. It did not slow the fleshless beasts.

And when they set upon him, their teeth felt like ice.

CHAPTER 1
SURVIVAL

It was still dark when Shane awoke. The sound of the waves crashing against the rocks was almost soothing, and it likely helped in getting to sleep the night before. He hadn't thought he would sleep, but it had taken both him and Frank.

No one had come looking for them, at least no one who had come down the snowy cliffside path that led to the cave in which they had spent the night. The blizzard had ensured that the villagers would hold tight in their homes, but that wouldn't last. Shane could already see that the snow had lessened. It fell now in simple, fat, fluffy flakes. It was almost serene, a sharp contrast to the brutal storm from the night before.

Frank was still asleep, curled up with blankets provided by the girl, Alina, from the village. The fire had died down to glowing, red embers. Shane pulled over another of the logs that had been waiting in the cave and set it down gently.

The way the stone passage curved in the cave, they were protected from much of the wind. The exterior had jutting, rocky barriers that stopped most of it before it reached the cave's mouth. It was an exceptionally well-laid-out space for withstanding a night in the cold. It almost seemed like it had been made intentionally.

They had come to Maple Grove Island to investigate the disappearance of a young man, the son of Frank's old army buddy. They had found the boy on the island, his remains torn apart and half-eaten. By what, they did not know at the time.

The community on the island, presenting themselves as a sort of hippie commune that made maple syrup and lived a peaceful, isolated life, knew about the ghost. Not all of them knew it was real. Not all of them knew it was a killer, but enough of them did.

The island's leader, Mallory, certainly did. She had sacrificed the young man, believing that the ghost was a nature spirit that would help their harvest and guarantee them abundance for the year. She was deluded and didn't want to hear otherwise.

Everyone had been more than happy to help Frank and Shane when they first arrived. Or at least pretended to. They lied, saying they didn't know about the young man. They said he had left the island, and that no one had seen him since. Things had changed quickly after that first day. The villagers had tried to burn them to death in their cabin and then chased them with guns through the woods.

If it wasn't for the fact that most of the residents of the island were incompetent and unskilled in fighting or tracking, and none of them could shoot a gun to save their lives, Shane would probably be dead. As it was, he was waiting out a blizzard inside a cave on the island's eastern rock wall.

There was no way to contact the outside world except by radio. The only radios that Shane and Frank knew about were on the three boats on the island's western shore. The boats were guarded by armed men.

Shane had promised a man named Mo, the ship's captain who'd taken them to the island days earlier, that they would contact him after three days. With the blizzard, Shane didn't think Mo would hold them to the agreement. It was unreasonable to expect that he would have come to them, or that they could somehow get to him. That meant it was unlikely anyone was looking for them. They needed to get away on their own. They needed to get to the boats.

Shane didn't want to leave. The entire island's population was looking to kill him. There were also mutilated ghosts that had been killing and trying to eat people, but Shane wanted to stay. He wanted to finish what they had started and destroy the spirit.

The problem was it was not just one ghost. Shane had destroyed one the night before, and it was not the ghost he had tangled with previously. He didn't know how many spirits were on the island, but he suspected there were several. Combined with the weather working against them, and the villagers, Frank was right. It would be smarter to head back to the mainland. Smarter to let the authorities know that the people of the village were murderers, or at least complicit to murder.

"We cannot police this island," Frank had said. Shane wanted to handle it, but Frank was right. Real people's lives were involved, some of whom were already dead and had families looking for them. They shouldn't have had to wait for Shane to decide how to handle the situation.

Frank had agreed with Shane, however, that they weren't done. The police in Maine could deal with the islanders, but the ghost was for Frank and Shane to solve. One ghost or several, it didn't matter. They would take care of it and make sure no one else who came to the island suffered the same fate.

Fire climbed up the side of the log, brightening the cave, and increasing the warmth in the small space. Alina, the girl who had brought the missing young man to the island in the first place, had spent the night there previously. She didn't remember how she'd gotten there, but Shane suspected one of the ghosts had taken her.

While ghosts were killing the villagers of the island and trying to eat their flesh, at least one of them was not acting like the others. Shane had fought with the ghost more than once, but it refused to commit to the fight. It backed off when it should have pressed advantages, and once, it even seemed like it helped them get away from armed men. Shane wondered if it had helped Alina escape, and if so, why.

There were still so many questions. The little village on the island had been built long before any of the people who lived there now. There were also unmarked graves in the woods, and what looked like a small altar of skulls hidden in the base of a felled tree. All of it looked to be well more than one hundred years old, probably even older.

Something horrible had clearly happened on that island. The victims of the ghosts were being killed in the same way the ghosts themselves had died. Their bodies were carved up with tools, but also with teeth. It was as though someone was preparing them to be used as meals, butchering the body, taking the largest muscles, and then chewing the bones clean.

Shane had never dealt with cannibals. He doubted many people had. While the ghosts could not eat their victims, that could very well have been what happened to them while they were alive. A cycle that repeated for years.

On an isolated island, maybe during the brutal blizzards that took place in winter, who knew what could have happened? It wasn't inconceivable that the original builders of the village resorted to the unthinkable if they were trapped.

Shane did not like to give in to speculation. There could have been a million explanations for everything on the island he didn't understand. Starting to make assumptions was how people like Mallory ended up believing that the ghost was a nature spirit and that allowing it to kill people would somehow produce more maple syrup for the islanders. Shane wouldn't ever give in to something that foolish, but the sentiment was the same.

He preferred to deal with concrete explanations. In the end, it also didn't matter to him. Why the ghosts did what they did was a secondary concern. They just needed to be stopped. If he never found out what happened on that island, he wouldn't lose a lot of sleep over it.

Shane had agreed to come with Frank to the island because Frank needed his help. Frank couldn't do what Shane could do. A ghost needed to be stopped, and that was what Shane planned to do.

Dawn was just breaking when Frank awoke, and the dark horizon became a pale gray. The sky was still filled with clouds, and it was unlikely they were going to see the sun.

Shane filled the small kettle that Alina had provided them with snow and boiled the water. They had brought coffee with them from the mainland, and they shared a breakfast of beef jerky and some crackers with it.

The men spoke little. They didn't need to. One of the things Shane appreciated about Frank was that he knew when a conversation was necessary and when one wasn't. They finished quickly and packed their things before heading out. Shane took the handgun from his pack before leaving, slipping it into the waistline at the rear of his pants. The people of the island were becoming more trigger-happy, and he wanted to be prepared.

There was every reason to believe that the docks would still be guarded. Nevertheless, they were prepared to square off with anyone who stood in the way. The night before, they had allowed one of the guards to get a flare off and summon help. It would not happen again.

With the blizzard and the continued cold temperatures, Shane didn't think more than two guards would be there. No one could handle being out in that weather for too long. They had to be working in shifts, and they would likely be miserable. The villagers were not fighters by nature. Most of them were the hippies they presented themselves as; they were just liars on top of it. These people weren't prone to violence, strategy, or anything that would help them keep Shane and Frank from the boats.

The narrow path up the side of the cliff to the island surface was buried beneath a foot of snow. Shane took the lead, clearing as much as he could out of the way. When they reached the top, the untouched blanket of snow stretched in every direction as far as he could see.

The maple forest before him was quiet and still. There were no animals or birds on the island. Nothing stirred. The snow fell softly, there was barely a breeze, and for one of the first times since they arrived, visibility was not terrible. It was just that there was nothing to see.

The world had an unfinished look to it in the dim light of early morning. The docks and the three boats were on the exact opposite side of the island. The snow was deep, and the going would not be quick, but it was their only option. Shane started forward and Frank followed behind.

They kept to the forest, avoiding the open field that existed between it and the village. Shane did not want to risk being seen either in the village or at the sugar shack. He also thought that perhaps the snow might not be as deep between the trees in parts of the woods, allowing them to go faster. There was a risk of running into the ghost, but it didn't seem to have any qualms about where it showed up on the island, so being in the trees would not necessarily make things worse.

There was a heaviness to the quiet of the island that was unnatural. Even the sea was muffled, the howling of the wind absent at long last, and the only sounds were their footfalls crunching in the snow.

Shane kept his eyes peeled for any signs of the ghosts. With any luck, he and Frank would be on a boat and leaving the island within the hour. It was too bad that he didn't put a lot of faith in luck.

CHAPTER 2

SILENCED

Shane and Frank were hunkered down in a small clearing they had made behind a copse of maple trees. They were about twenty yards from the path that led down to the docks on the island's western side.

There had been two guards stationed in front of the path the night before. Shane saw no one now, and that seemed suspicious. If Mallory knew Shane and Frank were trying to get to the boats, why would they leave them unguarded?

Initially, the people of the village had just wanted Shane and Frank to go away. They had told them the same lies that they had told the police who came looking for the young man named Jackson. He had been on the island, he didn't seem like a good fit, and he had left of his own volition. That was their official story, and the police had no reason to suspect otherwise.

The locals hoped Shane and Frank would believe the same story and also leave to find Jackson on the mainland. Things changed when it became clear that they weren't satisfied with simple answers. Eventually, Mallory decreed that Shane and Frank were not allowed to leave the island. Instead, they were to be executed. When burning down their cabin with them locked inside didn't work, the villagers were just going to shoot the men.

Leaving the boats unguarded smelled like a trap to Shane. Something was wrong. Mallory had some cunning. She would set a trap, and Shane could imagine it being clever.

The two men waited in silence, spying the path from around the trees where they were hidden. It was hard to tell from a distance, but it looked to Shane like there was no longer a footpath there. The snow had covered everything, which meant there had not been people there in some time.

"Nothing here," Frank said.

He had been watching the eastern side while Shane observed the west. The sun was fully risen now, and though the gray skies kept it at bay, the world was clear beyond the soft, fat flakes of falling snow. There was nowhere for anyone to hide unless they had ventured down the zigzagging path to the dock below.

It was likely that the guards had fallen back to the boats. It made sense during the blizzard that they would seek shelter. There was only one way to know for certain.

Shane nodded at Frank, and they got up, shouldered their packs, and then headed single file toward the nearly hidden path down to the dock. It was difficult to be stealthy in a field of white, especially when they had to clear their way.

Shane approached the western edge of the island and the rocky cliffside that led downward. He heard the ocean softly crashing against the rocks below. A small inlet came in toward the island, and it was there that the tiny wooden dock awaited with three boats. Or at least, that's what they had seen when they first arrived.

As Shane approached the edge, ready to head down to the zigzagging path, he got a clear view of the inlet and the dock below. The wooden slats were covered in snow, as were the rocks that jutted up to the left and to the right. There was nothing on the water. All three boats were missing.

Shane cursed, and Frank came to his side, looking down over the edge.

"Unbelievable," Frank said.

"No, I can see her doing something like this," Shane replied. "Mallory would cut off her own people at a time when they were being killed by this spirit, just to spite us. Just to keep us here."

"Sounds like her," Frank conceded.

Mallory had taken on something of a fanatical tone. She believed wholeheartedly in the spirit of the island. Shane did not doubt that she thought she was speaking the truth about what the spirit did for the people. She believed they were prospering, but she also believed she needed to give people to the ghost for that to happen. She was fine with human sacrifices to a cannibal spirit. She believed it was the greater good playing out. She was crazy, but she was crafty. She wasn't stupid.

"They can't have gone far. They must have moved them someplace we haven't seen yet. Some backup dock or cove somewhere."

"You don't think they just left?" Shane asked.

"I don't think she can afford to lose three loyal people who would need to captain those boats."

Shane nodded, considering Frank's words. He made a good point. The island's population was relatively small, only several dozen people. Among them, not everyone was on board with what Mallory was doing. Most of them seemed to be in the dark.

By Shane's count, Mallory only had between one and two dozen people loyal to her and backing her up. Those seemed to be the ones who were aware of the ghost and the price that they were all paying to be on the island. The rest were ignorant, simply living in an artsy community that made maple syrup.

"What should we do now? We could wait for Mo, but there's no telling if or when he could come, especially with the weather," Frank said.

Shane nodded. He didn't want to leave their fate in the hands of someone they barely knew. The missing boats were a setback. It wasn't just the boats; it was the radios. There was no way to contact Mo on the mainland, or anyone else. But Shane did not think that was the end of things.

There had to be another form of communication on the island. There had to be a way for people on the mainland to contact the boats when they were out. Someone had another radio. It didn't have to be big, it could be a simple handset, like a walkie-talkie. Something easy enough to hide in any of the buildings. Shane just didn't believe there was nothing else around; it didn't make sense. If they had a stock of hunting rifles on an island that had no game to hunt, they had to have communication tools.

"Someone on this island has to have a radio, a SAT phone, or something they can use to talk to the outside world. There's no way they leave it up to the boats. If there's an emergency in the village, does everyone run down to the boat to do something about it? Doesn't make sense," Shane said.

"You're right," Frank agreed. "But how do we find a radio? If anything, I would guess Mallory has it."

"I was thinking the same thing," Shane said. "So, we have to get it from her."

The cold was far more tolerable now that the blizzard had ended. Shane barely noticed as they changed direction again, heading for the village now, south of where they were observing the docks.

Leaving tracks was unavoidable, but they hoped that if anyone from the village showed up, it would be too late for them to do anything. Just to be safe, they took meandering paths and occasionally would split up to leave false trails before joining up again to ensure that any trackers would waste time coming after them.

The two men circled wide in the village, keeping low so that there was no chance anyone would see them. They stuck to the western edge of the island, which grew shorter the closer they got to the southern tip.

They saw smoke rising from the village but none of the cabins, thanks to the bowl-like depression in which the little village had been built. It kept the cabins hidden from sight until you were right upon them, but it also ensured that no one in town would see anyone coming until the last minute.

Shane's plan was to find the best position from which to observe the village. He wanted to get the lay of the land and see what everyone was up to. Then, they would need to find a way to approach Mallory's cabin. It was the most likely location for any kind of radio or phone. They would need time to search it, so a distraction would be in order. Something to draw her out, keep her busy for a while.

The village elder's home was full of shelves. There were drawers and cupboards and things crammed in every conceivable corner. She could have easily hidden a small radio anywhere, so they would need time to do the job thoroughly.

It would have been easy enough for Frank to set up a distraction and for Shane to break into the old woman's house. The cabins were not secure; he could have broken the rear window or just taken down the door. The problem was doing so when no one was looking.

None of that mattered by the time they got to the village. Shane's plan had to be put on the back burner as a scream cut through the chilled air.

It was a woman, possibly in pain but definitely terrified. Shane and Frank made their way to the edge of the bowl overlooking the village. The streets were empty. The several dozen little cabins were closed tightly, nearly all of them with smoke floating up in puffy, white clouds from the chimney. With the thick layer of snow everywhere, the image was almost serene if not for the woman in the center of the village near the stone altar.

One of the ghosts had grabbed her and was dragging her by a handful of hair. Shane vaguely recognized the woman, an artist in her sixties. He had been introduced to so many people and had not paid much attention to them at the time. It was clear from Frank's reaction, however, that he did recognize her.

"That's Miriam," Frank said softly. "She makes pottery. She's a good person."

The ghost was taking the woman away from the central hub of the town—the stone altar that was like the middle of the ramshackle wagon-wheel pattern of the whole place—and dragging her down a side path. Blood was splattered in the snow, but it did not belong to Miriam.

Someone else had suffered the same fate earlier.

Shane hadn't seen the confrontation begin, but no one else was coming out of their homes, and there was no way the people of the village weren't hearing the screams. They knew what was happening, and they were ignoring it. That made Shane think that Miriam was a sacrifice, something Mallory had convinced everyone would calm the spirit and ensure their prosperity. Because the ghost had taken so many people lately, Shane didn't know how much longer the villagers would believe lies like that.

"We have to help her," Frank said.

He was already moving, roughly sliding down the shallow hill that led into the village. Many of the pathways between cabins had been stomped down, well-trodden since the blizzard stopped, allowing quicker passage than if they circled through the deep snow on the outside.

Shane followed Frank. He wouldn't have gone head-first into the lions' den—there was every reason to believe they were at risk if they were seen by the villagers—but the other man wasn't wrong. The woman was going to die if they didn't do anything to help her.

The bloodstains in the snow became more prominent closer to the edge of the village where the ghost was dragging Miriam. The ghost was retracing its steps; it must have dragged one or two others that way since the blizzard ended. It seemed to want to take them into the woods rather than finish them in town, however, so at least that gave Frank and Shane some time.

Shane did not recognize the ghost that was taking the woman. It was not the one he had initially fought; it was another spirit that had suffered the same fate. His body was hacked apart, with whole muscles missing from his arms and legs. They weren't close enough to inspect him, but Shane had no doubt he was covered in teeth marks. Someone had feasted on the dead man's remains before he was dead.

The ghost moved swiftly through the snow. Unencumbered by the same physical body as the woman he dragged, he glided her across the surface while moving rapidly through the frozen blanket that covered the ridge and field beyond the little town.

Because he could move so swiftly, Frank and Shane struggled to catch up. They were already at a disadvantage of being on the far side of the village when they started. By the time they reached the edge of the bowl to climb out on the northern side of the town, the ghost was out of sight.

And Miriam's screams were fading.

CHAPTER 3
THE FEAST

Frank climbed the hill as fast as he could, with Shane right on his heels as they raced toward the forest, following the ghost that had already put a considerable distance between them.

Running in the foot-deep snow was not Frank Benedict's forte. Shane gave the other man a tap on the shoulder and passed him, following the shallow path created by Miriam being dragged across the surface. He pushed his way through, making it easier for Frank to follow.

As fast as Shane could go, he was nowhere near fast enough. The ghost had vanished beyond the trees, taking the woman with him. Frank and Shane were not even halfway across the field.

Neither of the men spoke. Shane was grunting from the exertion by the time he hit the tree line, sweat beading and then freezing on his forehead. Once in the trees, the going was easier, and he sprinted in long strides. He could no longer see the ghost, but Miriam's screams and his intuition told him where he needed to go.

The ghost had dragged the woman to the clearing in the center of the woods, the ring of unmarked graves partially buried in snow. Shane saw blood splatters and at least one more body next to the stones when he arrived.

Miriam shrieked as the ghost bit into her shoulder, growling like a dog. Shane hurdled the last snowbank to get into the clearing and stopped short, skidding through slick leaves, and nearly falling over.

A second ghost clambered from the snow, and then a third. All were mutilated, stripped to the bone, chewed up, and gruesome. Their wound patterns were slightly different, though: Some still had eyes. One was scalped, and one's nose was chewed off.

Two more spirits joined, and Shane took a step back, preventing Frank from entering the circle.

"We have to help her!" Frank pleaded as the new spirits joined the first. The woman's screams were bloodcurdling as half a dozen ghosts tore into her, using teeth and ragged fingers to tear flesh from every part of her body.

"Best thing we can do is let them finish quickly," Shane said.

There would be no saving Miriam. The second bite had torn through arteries in her neck. She was no longer screaming or fighting back.

The slavering, hungering ghouls attacking her made messy sounds as they chomped and gulped and tried to swallow the flesh they bit from her. The pieces of it simply fell to the ground underneath them, unable to be held up in non-corporeal bodies.

Blood and gummy chunks of muscle and skin hit the snow and congealed quickly, freezing in place before the mess could spread. Tissue clumped in gobbets that glistened and grew a frosty sheen.

The sound was both inhuman and not. The wet, slopping sound of torn flesh was something one might expect in a barn, like the sound of pigs released on the trough. But the sounds from the spirits—some of the only sounds Shane had heard them make—were all too human.

They sounded satisfied. The moans and hums of the famished, the obnoxious and unnecessary sounds a person makes when overreacting to a meal. It was almost theatrical, which made it even more vulgar. They continued as if they didn't notice that the food fell from their bodies. As if they were getting some form of sustenance from devouring the woman.

The scene was a unique kind of revolting. Shane had seen monstrous acts committed by the dead and the living alike. It wasn't the violence that he found off-putting, it was the joy the spirits seemed to experience. It was offensive in a way few things he had seen had ever been.

Each of these mutilated, broken, disgusting monsters was reveling in the act of devouring Miriam. The ones that still had eyes closed them in joy. It made a rage bubble deep inside Shane's gut.

He wanted to attack them. He wanted to tear the heads from every one of them, but he could not win a fight against six. One alone had been a challenge, and if any of them were as tough as the one he had fought the first time, he had no chance. He would be as dead as that woman in minutes, and Frank would soon follow.

There was no smart play in confronting the ghosts. They were already in danger because they were so close. If any of the ghosts decided that it had eaten its fill and turned its attention on them, it would be all over.

Shane and Frank dropped behind some of the maple trees, using the snowbanks for additional cover. If they left now, they would be seen. The best bet was to just stay out of sight and wait for the ghosts to finish.

Frank's anguish was unmistakable. He wanted to save the woman, even though she was long dead. He wanted to get the ghosts away from her body so she could at least retain some dignity in death. But all he did was join Shane in taking cover, getting out of sight so the ghosts would not see them.

Frank was smart. He knew a losing battle when he saw one. He didn't let emotion cloud his judgment, but that didn't mean he didn't feel it. It had been a long time since Shane saw someone look the way Frank had at that moment. It was more for the sake of who she was as a person, Shane thought. Frank looked like his heart was being torn in two.

Shane wondered how Frank did the job he did. Feeling so much, so intensely, had to make his work hard. When things worked out, and he resolved problems, it was probably very satisfying. But in cases like this—in cases where the ghost was not going to listen to reason, and it was more animal than human, maybe even more monster than animal—it must have been that much harder to feel things the way Frank did.

There was nothing for them to talk about, not that either man would have risked saying something. They sat behind the trees, ducked below the snow where they could occasionally look over at the ghosts, but mostly they just listened and waited.

The ghosts would have to stop at some point. The bodies they had seen so far had only been partially devoured. It was as though the ghosts somehow realized they'd had their fill and stopped.

It was impossible to ignore the vile slurping, lip-smacking, and moaning sounds. Shane focused only on the waiting. He wondered if Mallory or any of the other villagers knew how many ghosts were on the island. The way they spoke made it seem like they believed there was only one. If most of the villagers couldn't see them, they might legitimately think that.

It was also possible that Mallory was so deluded she wouldn't notice the difference between one ghost and another. Their wounds were certainly similar enough. And if she thought it was legitimately some sort of island spirit and not the deranged ghost of a man from a prior age, she might not even care. She might think it was just an affectation of the spirit's presence.

What confused Shane more than anything, though, was the nature of the agreement that existed between the villagers and the ghosts. Watching the spirits in action, he had no idea how anyone could have spoken with them enough to make a deal. These were not men; these were beasts. That a deal could exist didn't make sense to Shane. That people had lived on the island for years didn't make sense. Why weren't these ghosts killing everyone? Why hadn't they killed everyone long ago?

There was more to the puzzle that Shane had yet to discover. One ghost was different than the others. That one ghost seemed to have intellect and understanding. Maybe it had brokered the deal. But at the same time, Shane had not seen that one ghost kill anyone. It had fought him and could have killed him, but it didn't.

There was something more to the story of Maple Grove Island. Some reason why the dead were the way they were. And some reason that the people of the village were allowed to live, or at least had been until recently. It seemed like the ghosts' new killing spree was outside of the way things normally operated. If that was true, what had changed?

The sounds of the slavering, ravenous ghouls began to die down. Frank had not taken his eyes off the scene, but Shane had his back to it. He turned, peering around the edge of a maple tree and watching as one after another, the ghosts pulled away.

Some of the ghosts remained on their haunches, chewing slowly and lazily as though in a daze. It made Shane think of cringe-inducing jokes he'd heard about people being in food comas. It was as though they were lost in the idea of eating the woman's flesh. But eventually, as they swallowed, and the chunks of meat passed through their bodies to land in the snow, the ghosts turned and slinked away, disappearing into the shadows under the layers of snow.

Soon enough, all the ghosts were gone. What remained in the clearing was a slaughter. Blood and chunks of chewed meat were everywhere. What remained of the woman's body was torn apart and barely recognizable. They had been more violent with her than they had with the others. Their attacks had escalated. Very little flesh remained on the woman's bones, and what they had not chewed off, they had torn off.

There were none of the cuts in the style that existed on their bodies, no bladed tool had been used. It was just pure, bestial savagery. Shane doubted that a pack of wolves would have been any less gentle.

The snow was soaked red from stone to stone in the ring of graves. More of it was splattered beyond the ring, remnants of the other bodies that had been dragged out there. Since the ghosts could never truly be satisfied with what they were eating, there was nothing to make them wait for another kill. There was likely a very limited amount of time left for the people of the little village, whether they knew it or not.

The two men waited, watching the space and silence, taking the time to make sure the ghosts were gone. Shane got back to his feet when he was satisfied. They needed to get back to the village. They needed to find the radio that must have been hidden somewhere and contact the mainland or one of the boats.

There had to be a way off Maple Grove Island.

CHAPTER 4

WHAT WAITS

The walk back to the village was easier now that they could follow their tracks. They only followed the trail so far, though. Since the ghost had left with Miriam, it was likely that at least a few of the people from the village had ventured out of their homes. They would have seen Shane and Frank's tracks. If anyone got close enough to see that they were boot prints, they would realize the ghost hadn't made them. There was a chance someone would already be looking for them, so they could not head directly back.

Shane saw no one approaching in the open field. Visibility was still good, and the light snowfall was soft and manageable. Neither he nor Frank had much to say after what they had seen. What was there to discuss? They had sat by and watched a woman die. But they had no choice. The outcome would either have been the woman dying or all three of them dying. Still, it didn't make it any easier to deal with.

A new issue was creeping around the edges of Shane's mind. Frank wanted to leave to contact the police. Mallory and the others were letting people on the island die. They were essentially murderers. Shane didn't disagree that they deserved punishment, but he wondered if bringing new people to the island was a good idea.

If this became a full-blown police investigation, there would be detectives, uniformed officers, forensic teams, all kinds of media, and more. Most ghosts were happy to avoid the spotlight. That was why they secluded themselves in cemeteries, old houses, basements, and attics. But the ghosts on the island had never endured that kind of spotlight.

If the dead men on Maple Grove had been there as long as Shane thought, there was a chance they had almost no understanding of the modern world. The people on the island still lived as if it were a hundred years ago. If police showed up with cameras and radios and so many other people, the ghosts might become overwhelmed and attack everyone. Shane and Frank would be creating a slaughterhouse by bringing new people in.

"I think we might need a new plan," Shane said as they broke from their original path to head east.

"There's more of them than we thought," Frank said.

Shane nodded.

"Seven at least," he agreed.

"But our friend from the village seems to be separate," Frank said.

"Friend. Yeah." Shane wasn't ready to consider that ghost a friend yet, but it had not tried to eat him, so it had that going for it.

"Maybe you should head out if we find the boats or can get a hold of Mo. Get back to the mainland," Shane suggested.

They were circling wide of the village, and Frank came to a halt, staring at Shane with a look of bafflement on his face. Shane stopped as well after a few steps, looking back at his friend, and then scanning the horizon. They were out in the open, sitting ducks if anyone else was looking.

"That is a hell of a thing for you to say to me," Frank said.

"We've got a bunch of cannibal ghosts. They're barely human. This won't be an easy fight."

"Never thought it would be."

The irritation in Frank's voice was clear. Shane hadn't meant it to be insulting, but he understood how it could have been taken that way.

"If this goes sideways, we could both die," he explained.

"You don't need to tell me that," Frank said.

"And if I have to worry about you dying, it's going to make it harder for me to get my job done."

He could see Frank clench his jaw. The muscles in his face were tense, and his eyes narrowed slightly. It was about as angry as Shane had ever seen the other man, even though he said nothing. Shane appreciated what he must have felt. If someone had said that to him, he might have punched them in the face. That didn't mean Shane was wrong.

Frank was a good man and a good friend. He was good at what he did, too. But fighting was not one of the things he did. He might not have wanted to hear it, but he knew it was true. Wanting to be in a fight that you couldn't win wasn't a good idea. It wasn't brave; it was reckless. And it was likely to get them both killed. Shane was willing to hurt his friend's pride if it meant laying out the truth.

Shane didn't really want anyone's help. More people usually meant more problems. He could handle it on his own, he just needed strategy. He needed to hunt the ghosts before they hunted him. If he was clever and could separate them from the larger group like the one he had already destroyed, he could take them all out. One at a time, they would fall like dominoes.

Shane started moving again, forcing Frank to come with him if he wanted to continue the discussion. Frank had taken a purposeful breath, and Shane watched him calm himself down and take a moment before he responded.

"I'm here for a reason," Frank said. "The moment I feel I'm in over my head, I'll let you know, but I don't need you looking out for me. I wanted you here to help me, not run the show because I didn't think I could handle it."

"Understood," Shane replied.

They were still out of sight of the village, circling wide to the southeast past some scruffy-looking bushes. A shape crept out from behind several, moving on all fours, and then stopped directly in their path.

Shane recognized the ghost right away as the one that had been missing from the slaughter in the forest. The one he had already fought. Seeing it again, the differences between it and the ones in the woods were more pronounced. This one still had scraps of clothing attached to him. The cuts in the muscle on his bone were more pronounced.

The dead ones in the woods looked like they had been savaged. But this ghost had been butchered. Someone had taken their time with him, carefully cut pieces from him, as if they knew what parts would be best. Only after they had taken what they wanted had they torn at what was left over with teeth and claws.

Frank saw the ghost at the same time Shane did, ending their conversation immediately. The ghost watched them with a curious expression on his face like a dog unsure what a human was up to.

Shane wanted to spread out and get distance between himself and Frank so that the ghost did not have two targets directly ahead. The snow made it difficult to move around that easily, though. It was basically corralling them. If either man moved, their mobility would suffer greatly as a result.

"I'll watch your back," was all Frank said. Shane nodded, stripping off his gloves and tossing them to the other man.

"Come on, then," he said to the ghost.

The ghost was quick to oblige. It understood what Shane was saying and what he wanted. There was no hesitation as it bounded forward in a sort of jog to meet him in the field of snow.

They clashed like two wrestlers, head-to-head, hands on one another's shoulders holding each other back. The ghost clacked his teeth, threatening to bite Shane's face, but Shane let his feet slide back on the slippery snow, using the ghost's force against itself as he fell back and flipped the spirit through the air.

The ghost had an advantage on the terrain. Not only did the snow not slow him down, but he could simply pass through it. Shane had to force his feet to clear it out of the way, and when he fell, he sank into it. As a result, the ghost could easily slip in and out of Shane's grasp, making the fight that much harder.

Shane had already learned that trying to hold the ghost was a losing strategy. The slickness of its bones and the strange, ghostly substance that covered him and made him slippery as though he was dipped in oil was not something easily overcome. Instead, Shane used it to help ease the ghost from one place to another as he moved it and then struck at it with his fists or elbows.

Tumbling about in the snow was like an awkward dance between them. They were up for one moment, and then on the ground again, fists colliding with bones. Then, they reset as the ghost clambered away and got back to his feet.

The ghost clawed at Shane's side, but his hands could not penetrate Shane's thick coat. The spirit could have done it—a winter jacket was no more an impediment to a ghost than a brick wall—but so close to Shane's body, whatever allowed him to interact with the dead and confront them physically seemed to extend to what he wore.

It was only a momentary setback in the ghost's efforts, but it was enough. Shane rolled them to the side, forcing the ghost onto the ground in the clearing he had made in the snow. He was on the ghost in an instant, forcing it face-down to the ground as he pushed into the ragged small of the ghost's back. Much of the flesh had been stripped away from the ribs and spine on his upper back, but the lower back was still partially intact, and that's where Shane pressed his knee.

Even the slickness of the ghost's bones would not save it now. There was no place for the spirit to go. Shane had one of his arms pinned behind his back so he could not wrestle free. The back of his skull was exposed as Shane put his elbow against it and began to press down, applying pressure to the white bone.

He had barely begun to push with all his weight when the ghost chattered his teeth again and looked back, catching Shane in his peripheral vision.

"Wait," the ghost croaked.

It was the first word Shane had heard any ghost on the island speak. He had wondered if the ghosts had lost the ability. For all he knew, their tongues had been excised along with the other muscles that had been torn away and eaten. If not that, then the ghosts had gone so feral that they had lost human speech. But he was wrong.

"Please," the ghost said. His voice was rough, unlike anything Shane had heard from a living person. "If you kill me, everyone here dies."

CHAPTER 5

THE TRAPPER

Shane looked at Frank. The other man had stepped closer and crouched down, observing the ghost with his face pressed into the snow.

"Didn't think you were much of a talker," he said.

The ghost turned his eye to Frank, mustering up a bit of a growl in his throat.

"Talk is pointless," the ghost said.

"Humor us," Shane said. "Tell me why I shouldn't crack your skull like an egg."

"You want to save those people in the village. Without me here, they would have all died years ago. This place would have been a tomb, the way it was when I got here. If you want those people to live, you need my help."

"So, you're their guardian angel? Hell of a job you've been doing," Shane said.

The ghost growled again and shifted briefly. Shane thought he might be escaping, but he went slack again almost immediately.

"I've tried to get them to leave, but they won't go. They accepted this idea that killing someone once a year and sacrificing them was giving them a paradise they never found where they came from. They believe this is an ideal way to live. They believe this is the best way. There's no way to talk to someone like that. So yes, people die. It used to just be one person a year."

"Why do any of them allow that to happen? Why do the other ghosts now come for more?" Frank asked.

"Because all they know is hunger," the ghost explained. "They haven't been men since before I died. They're just animals. They don't think. So, if you train them to eat once a year, they will eat once a year. And that's how things worked until you came here. You've thrown off the balance, and they no longer have a routine. You destroyed one of them, and now they can't do their job, and I can't do my job."

Shane looked at Frank, and the other man shook his head.

"What job? What are you talking about? Who are you?" Frank asked.

"Will you let me up?" the ghost asked.

"You haven't given me a lot of reasons to trust your sincerity," Shane explained.

The ghost growled again.

"You have my word. I will not fight you."

"Charming," Shane said.

Frank put a hand on Shane's shoulder, out of view of the ghost. Shane sighed and eased up, taking his knee off the ghost's back and moving away. The spirit remained still on the ground until Shane had moved and then slowly pushed himself up, sitting on bony haunches once again and looking at the living men.

"My name is Frank. This is Shane."

"My name was Hugh Carson," the ghost said. "You should have never come to this place."

"What is going on here, Hugh?" Frank asked. "What happened to you and the others?"

Hugh sighed a softer growl and shook his head.

"I have been here for a long time. Over a century, last I heard the year. Our captain came here to explore the island as a potential outpost between Acadia and the Commonwealth. Our hull was gutted on the rocks, and we needed to make repairs. But a storm rolled in swiftly. We took refuge in the village there. Cabins, just a handful of them, kept us safe from the snow. Until they didn't. Men began to go missing. One after another."

"The dead were already here," Shane said.

"Those of us who lasted longer, who woke up each morning to discover more men missing, spoke of Wendigo sickness. Some of the men had heard of it from the native tribes we traded with in the deep north. The sickness that can turn a man into a monster and make him eat the flesh of the dead."

"You think that's what happened?" Shane asked.

"No," the ghost said. "This was no myth. Just monsters."

"Monsters," Frank said. "These other spirits. The older ones."

"I didn't see them until they came for me that night. They were as you see them now. Monsters. Nightmares. I had never been so scared. They dragged me to the forest but soon abandoned me there. I thought I was free until another approached in the dark."

"Another?" Frank asked.

"If he had a name, I do not know it. The others do not speak. Nor does he. But he is strong and merciless. He had a weapon, a blade made of bone, and he cut into me while I still lived. He peeled the meat from my bones while I screamed until the pain was more than I could bear."

Hugh went silent then. Blood loss probably set in and knocked him out, Shane thought. Sliced apart by a spectral blade and then filleted. Cut to pieces like a roast. And the leftovers formed who Hugh Carson was now.

"But you came back," Frank said after a moment.

The ghost made a sound, and his expression soured.

"If that's what this is," he agreed. "Something came back. Something with my mind. My memories. Not by choice, I can assure you."

"I imagine not, no," Frank said. "But you said you do a job here."

"I have been fighting off the madness of the others for longer than I was ever alive. More than three times longer than I was ever alive, by my count. They work to keep the other one in check. Alone, they fear him. But they learned that as a group, they can overpower him. Like a pack of weaker wolves taking on the stronger. Numbers give them strength. Give them power. And while they focus on him, I could focus on them. I could keep them away from the people who kept coming here. Stop them from killing the way they killed me and my crew."

"Except for the few they manage to drag into the woods," Shane said.

Hugh grunted, aggravated by the insinuation.

"It is not by my choice. This woman they all follow let a man die when she arrived here. Offered him up in exchange for her life. And when it worked, she thought she'd made a connection. Summer came, and this place prospered and grew, and she thought she'd done it herself. As if this land wasn't green and full of life every summer," the ghost explained.

Shane glanced at Frank again but neither of the men spoke. Mallory had been killing since she got to the island. She made up this fantasy of the island spirit almost right away, using the cannibals to fill in the blanks in her mind.

It made sense in a perverse way. If the other spirits were more like a pack of dogs than men, why would they bite the hand that fed them? If they could still learn and understand things, they had grown accustomed to Mallory. They knew she would keep feeding them. And if they had gone years without anyone being on the island, they could still be smart enough not to ruin a good thing. It was against their best interest to kill everyone, or at least it had been.

"Soon enough, if something went wrong, if storms ravaged crops or the weather was too poor for getting sap from the trees, she staked out someone new and said it was for the island. The others ventured in and took the sacrifice. Even I cannot keep them from a body willingly offered. It has been that way ever since. Until now."

"Until we destroyed one," Frank said.

Hugh grumbled and shifted on his haunches.

"They work in patterns. They patrol the forest. Usually, they don't cross the field unless they've been alerted to someone staked out, sacrificed. But with one missing, they can't follow their patterns. It is like one gear taken out of a clockwork. The others might still spin, but the machine is no longer working properly."

"And so, this other ghost?" Shane asked.

"He's already seen the holes. He's already appeared. He knows he can't fight six of them, but he knows six of them can't cover the ground that seven used to."

"Who is this ghost? Why do they fear him?" Frank asked.

"I do not know. He is not like them. But he eats. He savages victims. I think he was their killer. He is the reason they are all dead, so they both fear and hate him. But he is powerful. It is all they can do to keep him at bay."

"They protect the village from him?" Frank asked.

"No," Hugh said. "They have no care for the living. They keep him at bay so that he cannot feast on them. He has no care that they are dead. He will devour them. They are all that's left. There were more when I first arrived, but they had not banded together yet, so he took advantage."

"But there are only seven graves," Shane said. "Seven graves for seven ghosts."

Hugh shook his head.

"Those graves are not theirs. They had no graves. Who would have buried them? They are simply the seven who remained. Perhaps they adopted the stones symbolically. I don't know. I don't care."

Shane grunted, pulling a cigarette from the pack in his coat pocket and lighting it. Hugh watched him curiously while Shane took a moment, looking from the ghost to Frank and back.

"So, I threw a monkey wrench here. Now what? This boss ghost is going to start picking off the half-eaten crew?"

"He will kill everything on this island, living or dead. There is no way to stop him."

Hugh seemed confident in his assessment of the ghost's abilities. Shane was less convinced. He had met plenty of ghosts that were positive of their superiority in the past. None were still around. But Shane was. No ghost was indestructible; they just got used to thinking they were because they had not found anyone who could destroy them. Shane was more than happy to be an enlightening influence in their afterlives.

Hugh smirked, looking at Shane.

"You think me wrong," the ghost said. It wasn't a question, but Shane chose to answer, nonetheless.

"Just because you haven't destroyed this ghost doesn't mean he can't be destroyed."

"I've seen what you can do. You surprised me when we first fought. I had never experienced anything like that. I did not think the living could do what you do. But you couldn't even destroy me. How could you hope to destroy him?"

Shane exhaled a cloud of smoke, squinting as a light breeze blew it back into his face, and stared at the ghost.

"Did you forget what just happened before this conversation started?" Shane asked. "The only reason you're still here is because you begged me not to destroy you. And I thought it would be a good idea to listen to what you had to say."

Hugh chuckled, adjusting his footing, and setting one bony hand on the ground to steady himself.

"I never tried to kill you. Even from that first fight, I was never trying to kill you. I wanted to scare you off. I wanted to convince you to leave this island and maybe save your lives."

"Taking it easy on me, then." Shane grinned.

The ghost shrugged, an awkward gesture given how much meat was missing from his upper arms.

"This thing has never spoken to me. I have seen it before in passing. It is not so much like a man anymore. Not the way the others are. They are like dogs. They think and act like hungry beasts. He is not like that."

"Meaning?" Shane asked

"Meaning," Hugh continued, "he's like something else. Something beyond a man or a beast. I think, a long time ago, he was among the men who built those stone cabins. I think those men suffered the same fate as everyone who came to this island for a long time after that. There was nothing to eat. The rocks had destroyed their ship. And the weather grew worse."

"You think he resorted to cannibalism. Which fits what we've seen," Frank said.

Hugh shook his head.

"You misunderstand. Everyone else who came here has had to face the dead. But these first men were alone. That means, if they resorted to killing and eating one another to survive, one man would be left in the end. One man would survive, eating the bodies of his fallen companions. Until, eventually, he died as well. Alone, surrounded by the atrocities he had committed."

"The Cannibal King," Shane said, taking the last puff of his cigarette. "So, you're saying he's utterly mad."

CHAPTER 6
FOR YOUR LIVES

"Without the seven to overpower this king, as you call him, he will be free to roam. He will kill everyone. Even if you think you can stop him, and even if you're right, people will still die. And I do not think you are right," Hugh explained.

The trio had moved closer to the village. Shane did not trust Hugh yet, but the ghost was being communicative, and he was not fighting, so Shane was willing to give him the benefit of the doubt.

His story did not offer much useful information. Some background, perhaps, but Shane gleaned nothing useful from it. There were no secrets that would give them an edge in a fight. They already knew the other ghosts seemed more like animals than men, so there was nothing practical there. The information about this Cannibal King was new, but also not very beneficial in terms of strategy.

If they came across the ghost, Shane knew to be wary, but it wasn't as though he would offer to shake his hand upon meeting, anyway.

"We have to get these people out of here," Frank said.

Their plan was being forced to evolve yet again. From an effort to go to the mainland, to wanting to destroy the cannibal spirits, to now evacuating the island. Shane had no interest in saving the lives of Mallory and her followers. But, by the same token, he was not going to disagree with Frank that letting them stick around and be cannon fodder was a good idea. Especially those like Alina or Clint who had done nothing to become a part of what was happening.

The problem was that they were back to the same issue they'd had previously. They needed the boats, and they were missing. Shane was certain that Mallory was in charge of the boats, which meant they had to convince her that it was in her best interest to leave the island along with everyone else. They had to convince the woman who was willingly sacrificing people to hungry, wolflike cannibal ghosts that she needed to do the right thing.

"She's going to fight this," Shane said.

They were just beyond the bowl in a hiding place they had used the day before, under the cover of some shrubs from which they could look down into the village. Smoke rose from most of the chimneys. People were out and about now that the storm was over. Most of them were acting like it was any other day, as if Miriam had not just been dragged kicking and screaming into the forest by a ghost.

"I know," Frank said, "but we don't need to talk exclusively to Mallory. Everyone here has seen what has happened. We can let them make their own decision."

"And if they elect to stay behind?" Hugh asked.

"If anyone chooses to stay here and die, we can't do much about that," Shane said. "Our duty is to give them the choice. I think that's more than fair."

Shane could tell Frank was still frustrated with the idea. If Frank had his way, he would bring Mallory and her followers just as readily as everyone else. Frank was no foolish idealist; he would happily turn her over to the authorities. But he would rather bring her to the mainland and save her from being eaten. Shane was less committed to that plan.

The bigger issue than convincing Mallory or her people that they were in danger was convincing them not to kill Shane and Frank. If they couldn't get past that, then convincing anyone that their sacred island spirits were just feral, insane cannibals was a non-starter.

Frank turned to Shane, his breath misting as he nodded toward the village.

"I know you don't necessarily agree with this. You don't want to help these people, or not all of them. But Mallory has been lying to them, we need to remember that. I don't think these are bad people. I think a lot of them were hurt or broken, and this was an accepting place for them. It's hard for them to believe bad things about it."

Shane simply nodded. Frank was more optimistic than he was. That was fine. That was Frank's wheelhouse. Shane would be there to back up whatever play he chose. But if things went sideways, he would be ready.

He glanced at Hugh. Unlike either living man, the ghost seemed to have no interest in the village. He watched Frank and Shane, not the people below. Shane hoped he wasn't making a mistake by offering his trust, however limited, to the ghost.

Hugh's story was a unique one, and hard to believe at some points, but that didn't mean Shane thought he was lying. The ghost, a former trapper, was not given to the sorts of affectations Shane found with ghosts that spun stories or deceived. He seemed to be a simple man, or the ghost of one. Shane believed he was telling the truth, at least how he understood it.

"We need to avoid Mallory and get as many others as we can first," Shane said. "Get Alina, maybe Clint. Have them tell others."

"I will watch for the spirits," Hugh said. "They have already taken people today. They are emboldened now. They might come for more."

Shane nodded and left the ghost to it. He tapped Frank on the shoulder, and the two men left together. The ghost had already vanished, slipping below the snow and lurking out of sight.

The men descended from the edge of the bowl into town at the southeast corner. There was the least amount of activity at that corner of the town, and little reason for anyone to be at the rear of the cabins.

They made their way to Alina's home first. The snow behind it was undisturbed. No one had left out of the rear entrance since the blizzard.

Shane tried the back door of the cabin, knocking and then twisting the handle. The village cabins did not have locks, and if anyone wanted to bar the door, they would have to do so from the inside while they were there. Alina's door opened easily, showing the empty cabin within. A low fire, barely more than embers, burned in the fireplace offering warmth.

There was no sign of the young woman inside. She might have already gone to have her morning meal, or maybe she was staying with someone else after the events of the previous night. The village was not large, though. They would find her sooner or later.

Securing the door, Shane looked around the edge of the cabin toward the interior of the village. He was not sure which of the people in town were loyal to Mallory and which were not. They would have to risk going out where others could see them to alert everyone to what was happening. To let them know Mallory had been lying to them, and that people were going to keep dying.

"Look," Frank said.

They were at the edge of Alina's cabin, looking down one of the roads that followed an erratic path toward the town's central hub in the altar that was planted there. Though the way was not perfectly straight, and some later cabins had been built at odd angles that overlapped, Shane saw a man walking not far from them, tall and skinny, with a long scarf around his neck.

"Clint," Frank called out.

The other man turned his head, searching until he caught sight of Frank waving him over. Clint smiled and then looked unsure for a moment. He looked around, as though expecting someone was following him or listening in, and then walked quickly toward the back of Alina's home.

"It's so good to see you guys." For a moment, Shane feared the man would hug him. "I thought you would have been goners for sure in that storm after what happened."

The villagers had tried to burn Shane and Frank to death in their cabin before they escaped into the night. After that, Blaine and some of his friends had hunted them through the woods, but that had not worked out for them.

"It was close. Blaine tried very hard to kill us," Frank said.

Clint's expression changed from happiness and relief to something much darker. The smile left his face, and he lowered his head.

"Blaine's gone now," he said quietly.

"Gone?" Shane asked.

"It happened last night. The island came for him."

Shane glanced briefly at Frank and then returned his focus to Clint.

"It killed him?"

"Think so," Clint said. "I heard him screaming. I wanted to go to him, but Mallory said you can never go out when the island comes. You can never see it because it will take you, too. And his screams got quieter and quieter, and then he was gone. I thought it was done, but it came back later for Ms. Miriam."

"You heard that as well?" Shane asked.

Clint nodded and avoided eye contact.

"I know Blaine was not a nice man. Especially to both of you. I've never seen him that angry, and he could be pretty mean. But Ms. Miriam was a very nice lady. Everyone loved her; you can ask anyone. I don't know why it had to be her."

"It didn't have to be her, Clint," Shane said.

The taller man looked at him finally, confusion on his face.

"This island spirit—spirits, plural—Mallory told you about isn't what she said. These things aren't making your lives better. They want to kill you. All of you. Everyone on Maple Grove. And they're going to unless we can get you all out of here."

Clint's expression became very awkward, very pained, and he shook his head.

"No, guys… come on. I shouldn't even be talking to you. Mallory will get so angry."

"Clint," Frank said. "You said Miriam was good. I met her, and I liked her, too. Did she deserve to die?"

"No, but the island—"

"How many will it take, Clint?" Shane took his attention back. "It took Jackson, Blaine, and Miriam. How many others? How long will the rest of you last at this rate?"

"Mallory says it's because of you guys," Clint said reluctantly. He was like a child being forced to admit he had done something wrong, Shane felt a minor pang of sympathy. Clint was a big guy. To an outside observer, he looked like he might be tough, but he was very naïve inside. "She said the island is angry because you're here. If you guys go away, it will stop."

"It will not stop, I promise you that," Frank said. "This is not us."

Clint shook his head again.

"Most of the guys who went out last night never came back. People are blaming you for it. They think it was you that killed Blaine and, I don't know, maybe Miriam, too. It's really bad, you guys. You need to go."

"Do you know what happened last night?" Shane asked. "Does anyone know? We found one of the spirits out there, Clint. One of the ghosts that haunts this island. It's just a man. They're all just men who lived here a long time ago. They went mad, and they ate each other, and now their ghosts haunt this land trying to kill and eat anyone else who shows up. That's what's in store for all of you."

Clint's expression told Shane everything he needed to know. He hadn't thought Clint had the full story of what happened. He didn't think anyone knew about it, especially if Blaine was dead. But Clint was in the dark about the ghosts, about what they were doing, and about everything. Shane might as well have told him that Bigfoot had come and killed the others. Mallory's lie was so complete that he doubted anyone in the village had even a clue what was happening.

"Is Mallory here right now?" Shane asked.

"Of course," Clint answered.

"Good."

Shane looked at Frank. It was time to have a talk.

CHAPTER 7
THE DRAGON'S DEN

Shane headed down the same path Clint had traveled to reach them. Most of the snow had long since been trampled by others in the village, so once they were in the heavily trafficked areas, it was easy enough to move quickly. Frank and Clint followed him. Shane could see that this was not the way Frank wanted to do things. Shane would not stand in the way of Frank doing what he wanted, but for his part, he wanted to see Mallory as soon as possible. His patience had just about worn thin.

Plumes of gray-white smoke rose from the chimney of Mallory's little stone cabin next to the greenhouse. Shane did not pause at the door, he simply took the knob in hand and pushed it open, walking into the single, main room that took up most of the space.

Many of the villagers had packed into Mallory's place, sitting on chairs they must have brought from their homes or leaning against the walls and shelves to fill the space. More than a dozen people were there, which must have constituted the village elders and others who had been around Maple Grove the longest.

There were gasps as Shane entered, assorted hushed whispers between those closest together. Expressions twisted in surprise, anger, and upset that he had come in without knocking. Upset that he was there.

Mallory's expression was pure shock at first when he entered, soon tempered with rage at the intrusion. Or maybe it was anger at realizing Shane was still alive. He didn't particularly care.

A smoky haze filled the room, not just from the fire, but from candles and incense burning. They were living up to the hippie vibe, the lie they told themselves about the island. The lie that had lured in people like Jackson Raines and convinced them it was a good place to live.

The smell of it set Shane's teeth on edge. Not that it was offensive or that he wasn't used to smoke. It was just the pretense. The stupid reality that all these people were living while their friends were being murdered right under their noses. And for what? The promise that they would have lots of maple syrup? Of all the stupid lies he had heard people tell themselves, for some reason, that one stoked his rage.

Shane wanted to slap every one of their faces as they stared at him in shock for barging in uninvited. That they had the nerve to be offended by his sudden presence was enough to make him want to curse every one of them while he was at it. But he had bigger things to worry about.

"You do not belong here." Mallory glowered, barely concealing her rage. Two of her men, Blaine's backup thugs, moved to take him. Shane reached into the waistline of his pants at the back and retrieved the gun he had placed there when he and Frank had left the cave that morning.

The closest man, shorter and older than Shane with an uneven hairline, froze as Shane extended the gun into his face. He was less than two feet away, and Shane aimed right between the eyes. As tough as the man wanted to seem, he lost any semblance of it with a gun in his face.

There were collective gasps throughout the room. People backed up, holding each other and cowering away. There were no fighters in Maple Grove. Mallory and the others could get as angry as anyone else. They could have as much hate in their hearts, but none of them had trained for violence. None of them had the skill to back up their impulses.

"Tell them what's happening," Shane said, looking at Mallory.

The older woman's jaw was clenched so hard that Shane thought she might break her teeth. Her eyes were narrow, staring furiously at him. She looked like she might kill him with her bare hands if he had not had a gun drawn. It made him want to laugh.

"What are you talking about?"

"Tell them the truth about the ghosts of this island. About what happens when you leave someone out there to die."

Mallory looked at him like he was a fool. She shook her head, her anger merging with pitying disgust.

"Is that what you think you're doing here? Catching me in what? A lie? They all know, Mr. Ryan. I have never lied to these people."

Shane grinned broadly. Frank was watching the door behind him, and Clint was standing in place and shifting from foot to foot, looking extremely nervous and upset.

"Have you told them you made a deal with a cannibal? You let someone die so you could live? You keep putting people out for the monsters just so you can stay alive."

There was clear confusion among the others, but Mallory looked baffled by the words coming out of Shane's mouth. She looked offended, confused, and disgusted all at once.

"What absurd stories are you peddling here?"

"There is no island spirit. There are ghosts. Your island is haunted by dead men. Men who were murdered and eaten generations ago. When you feed them, when you kill your people to satisfy these things, it does nothing for you. The sap will flow from the trees no matter what. Your gardens will bloom or die no matter what. You have been killing people for no reason. Every person who has died on this island died for no reason."

"You have no idea what you're talking about," Mallory spat. "You spend three days here, and you think you know what we have built over years and years of hard work? You think you understand our sacrifice, our dedication? Who are you to know anything?"

"Shane's telling the truth," Frank offered, not to Mallory but the others. "I didn't lie to any of you people. I do this for a living. I help people because I can talk to the dead. I see them. I hear them. I can give and receive messages. And the dead on this island have no magical powers. They have no interest in helping you. They are just lost souls, angry and hateful. And they will keep killing until you are all dead in those woods."

There was scattered whispering, and that enraged Mallory even more. That anyone would listen to Frank and Shane was distressing her, which increased her anger exponentially. Shane saw her face flush red, and she was practically vibrating with it.

"The only reason many of us are alive today is because of this island." Mallory's voice was cold and flat. "We had nothing back where we came from. We had less than nothing. If I had stayed where I was, Mr. Ryan, I would have been beaten, broken, forgotten, and dead. I was less than nothing. This island gave me a life I never thought I deserved, and I will be damned if I let someone like you take that away from me. No one will take my life away from me ever again!"

Shane knew the woman was angry, but the fervor in her voice and the unmasked hatred she projected at him was more than he expected. For the first time since they had met, Shane experienced a moment of doubt. Mallory believed what she was saying.

Frank had told him, but it didn't ring true. He thought it was too absurd. How could anyone believe they were doing good for themselves or others by feeding them to mangled, monstrous things in a forest? But she believed it.

"I save lives here. The cost is high, but the cost of everything is high. It is one we are all willing to pay, and you have no right to destroy it."

She hissed the last words at him. Shane shook his head. She wasn't deceiving these people, not willingly, not in the way Shane had thought. Something had broken Mallory's mind somewhere in her past. Something had convinced her that there were acceptable levels of horror. Levels of sacrifice and pain. She had made the island a place where the death of a few was an acceptable sacrifice for the peace of many. Even if they could have found the same thing on any other island without the death involved. It was just that none of them tried, so none of them knew.

So, Mallory was not lying, not in her mind, anyway. Shane didn't care.

At the end of the day, whether she was deceiving them and leaving them to their death, or sincerely doing it, Jackson was dead. Miriam was dead. That idiot Blaine was dead. Who knew how many others were dead? All because one woman could not see reality, so she made up one that fit a story in her head.

"You can all believe what you like," Shane said, "but I know many of you saw the ghost that appeared in the storm. If you think that was a benevolent spirit, then go ahead and think that. If you think it's normal that at least three of you have died since I've been here, go ahead and think that, too. But I want you to look around the room. Look around your little village and do a head count. If three of you die every day, how much longer will you have a village? How much longer until one of you is next? Until all of you are gone?"

"It doesn't work that way," Mallory grated.

"Tell that to Miriam," Shane said.

There was more murmuring from the others in the room. More whispers and glances. Mallory might have been able to convince them that someone like Jackson was an acceptable sacrifice. No one knew him that well, and it was human nature to feel less attached to a stranger. But Miriam was one of them. People knew her and liked her, and it was much easier for all the people in that room to put themselves in her shoes than Jackson's. That was where Mallory had gone wrong.

"If you stay here, you will die." Frank addressed the others. "It is that simple. There are no forest gods here, just the ghosts of dead men who were trapped on this island. The men who built these cabins you live in, whose ships ran aground on the rocks, and who couldn't escape. You can repeat history or not. You can come with us and leave. And live."

It was about as harsh as Frank had gotten with these people. Shane was happy to hear it. They needed a dose of reality, and if they trusted Frank more than they trusted him, it was what they needed to hear.

"No one will believe your lies," Mallory said.

"No?" Shane asked. "None of you saw that ghost? Cut to pieces and chewed up? None of you wonder who built these cabins or what happened to them? You never see things from the corner of your eye on this island? Feel the air get cold for no reason?"

"Never heard stories of Wendigo sickness?" Frank added.

"I saw it," one of the people in the cabin said. A woman, near in age to Mallory, with hair the color of straw cut short and left spiky. She wore thick, gaudy bracelets and had numerous gold rings in both ears. "I saw that thing in the storm, Mallory. It looked like a nightmare. Is that the spirit you talk about?"

Others begin to speak up, asking Mallory questions about what they had seen. What Shane and Frank had said. Mallory ignored them all. She only had eyes for Shane.

And they were full of malice and hate.

CHAPTER 8

A GRAVE MISTAKE

"Put that gun away."

Mallory's tone was cold and severe. She was a woman used to being obeyed. She had power and seniority on the island and her position there had never been questioned. Why would it be? What kind of power grabs existed in a world of artists and gardeners and maple syrup?

The others in the cabin acted as if told to freeze by the police. They were as still as statues, their faces like those of scolded children. No one wanted to move or speak. Mallory's anger must have been a thing they had seen before. Or maybe it was the opposite. Maybe no one had seen it, and now, they had no idea what to do. In any event, it didn't seem as though the assembled rabble of the village would rise to the occasion and speak out against its de facto leader.

Mallory did not care for Shane's defiance. For wielding a gun that kept her and the others in check. It forced them to listen to him, listen to the truth, rather than allow her to steamroll everything as she was so clearly used to doing.

"This is a place of peace. It is you who brought violence. You are the reason for the horror that has befallen us. For the pain and the death. None of this happened until you got here," Mallory insisted.

"Except for Jackson Raines," Frank said. "And the other dead in the forest. Their bodies were torn apart and half-eaten. They all died before we arrived. Because of what you're doing."

"You understand nothing," Mallory hissed. Despite her diminutive stature compared to Shane, her anger had won out. She was no longer intimidated by the weapon he held. She had been standing on the far side of her small dining room table, but she rounded it now, pulling back the man with the strange hairline that Shane had been pointing the gun at, and took his place.

Shane had to adjust his aim. Mallory was short, and he lowered the weapon so it was level with her. She approached it readily until Shane very nearly had the barrel pressed on her forehead.

"Put that gun away now," she demanded.

"Funny, never heard you say that to Blaine or his guys when they were taking shots at me," Shane told her.

"Put that gun away," she repeated.

Her tone was harsh, but the volume was lower. She enunciated the words carefully, giving them strength. It was less like she was speaking and more like she was spitting something foul from her mouth with each word.

It had been some time since Shane felt that much hate from someone. Especially someone who he had not even particularly wronged. He hadn't been polite to the woman, but she hadn't deserved it. Usually, people who were in the wrong—people who had murdered others—didn't commit so fully to their emotional responses because they knew they were wrong. Mallory didn't have that luxury, or burden, depending on how one looked at it.

Shane kept his hand steady. Mallory's teeth were clenched, her lip was curled, and she took that final step. She pushed her forehead against the barrel, leaned into it, and Shane held firm. He let her press her face into the barrel of the gun, digging into her forehead hard enough to leave a mark.

"A long time ago, I promised myself that no man would ever threaten my life again. I've asked you more than once to put that gun down, and you've ignored me. I gave you every chance to look around this island. I let you stay in one of our homes. I let you eat our food. You have done nothing but spit on me since you arrived. I will not allow that any longer," Mallory said. "You brought this on yourself."

Shane was going to say something smart, some dig that he had half-formed in his mind at the expense of the woman, but there was no time. Older though she might have been, smaller, and certainly less intimidating, she had one thing going for her. Her height made it hard for Shane to see her hands. They were low to the ground relative to his, and he was focused on the barrel of his weapon, focused on her face, not what was happening below his waist.

The wide blade of a kitchen knife slashed up and in, catching the edge of Shane's hand but then sliding across the sleeve of his winter jacket preventing any serious damage. It was not an especially sharp knife, but it was sharp enough to dig into the meat near where he held the gun.

The others in the cabin gasped. Some were on their feet, and one of the men who originally came for Shane shouted something at the others. Shane was barely paying attention to them. The metal of the dulled blade dragged across the back of his hand. Flesh spread apart allowing blood to flow, and the wound went almost all the way to his wrist. It could have done some serious damage if the knife had been sharper, but it did enough to cause Shane to loosen his grip just as Mallory's other hand came up to pull the gun away.

Shane caught the woman's wrist but not before she managed to pry the gun loose. They fought briefly, and the gun fell to the floor as he took hold of her, preventing her from causing any more damage. She did not have the strength to resist him, and soon, the knife clattered to the floor as well.

The other people in the cabin were moving. Now that Shane was unarmed, they pushed past him to get past Frank and out the door. There was shouting, and Shane was knocked aside. He lost his grip on Mallory and scanned the floor for his weapon.

Mallory had found her knife again and came for Shane a second time. He couldn't see where his gun had gone; someone had either kicked it or picked it up. He had no time to worry about it as he had to defend against Mallory's next strike, a clumsy overhand stab. He caught her arm again, twisting it, and turning her around.

It was never Shane's intention to harm the woman; he just wanted the others to understand what she was doing. He was certain she deserved justice, but he didn't feel the need to engage in combat with an elderly woman. Nonetheless, she refused to submit easily and struggled against him even with her arm pinned behind her.

"Hold still or I will break it," he warned her.

"Then do it," she shot back, still fighting to get free.

"Stop!"

It was the man Shane had pointed the gun at to begin with. He was several paces back now, and the gun was in his hands. He was aiming at Shane and Mallory, and his hand was shaking. His face had gone pale, and his eyes were wide. He was terrified, but he had the gun.

Mallory continued to struggle in Shane's grip, and someone in the room screamed when they saw the gun had returned.

"Kill him!" Mallory shouted. She pulled hard, throwing her weight into escaping from Shane. But she didn't have the weight behind her, or the power. Shane's grip was solid, and she went nowhere.

The sound was deafening in the small space. The stone walls did not absorb the percussive force of the gun; instead, they reflected it back at everyone. There was a ringing in Shane's ears, and now everyone was screaming.

Frank had been trying to keep people in the cabin and stop the panic, but the villagers knocked him over in the snow and several of them ran, panicked and screaming, into the frosty air.

Even before the ringing died down, Shane knew what had happened. The man had pointed the gun at him, but he was not skilled with a weapon. His aim was poor, his arm was shaking, and Mallory refused to stay still.

Shane felt her go limp in his grasp. The arm he had been holding still behind her bent as she collapsed. Had the old woman not been there, the shot would have taken Shane in the gut.

He let her fall into a heap at his feet. He stepped over her, moving swiftly as the man who fired the gun stared in shock, frozen by the gravity of what he had done. Shane grabbed the weapon and simultaneously threw a punch with his other hand. He took the man hard in the jaw, causing his head to snap back and to the left. He fell hard, didn't even put his hands out to slow his fall, and hit his head on the ground. He was unconscious as Shane stood over him with the gun.

"Mallory!" It was the same blonde woman who had questioned her only moments earlier. "Mallory!"

She fell to her knees at the older woman's side and rolled her over. Her hands shook as she inspected Mallory's body. They came away soaked in blood from the bullet wound in her chest. The blonde woman sobbed, her cries coming shaky and broken as she struggled to breathe.

Others stood around crying, processing the shock of what they had seen, while many of those who had already fled had returned to the door, seeking cover from the stone walls but peering in past Clint and Frank to see what had happened.

"Somebody, please! Do something!" the woman begged.

No one moved except for Frank. He pushed past several of the villagers and got to his knees next to Mallory, ignoring the woman crying over her. Shane crouched as well, giving Frank room to work.

Mallory was still alive, but her breathing was weak and raspy. Bubbles came from the wound in her chest as Frank exposed it, stopping the bleeding as best he could.

"Someone get me some towels, a cloth, something." He spoke to no one in particular.

With the wound exposed, Shane saw it had entered Mallory's chest near her heart. It had obviously missed that organ but had hit her lung. Frothy blood came out of the wound as Frank pressed his palm against it, pushing down firmly as he waited for someone to get the towel he had asked for.

"Do you have a doctor in this town? A nurse? Medical supplies of any kind?"

No one answered him, and Frank lifted his head to the collective faces.

"Do you have medical supplies?" he shouted.

"I have... there's a med kit," the blonde woman stammered. "In the Great Hall."

"Get it," Frank instructed.

The woman stared at him, and he returned her gaze. The fog cleared from her eyes, and she turned to the door.

"Clint, get the medical kit from the Hall. Please hurry," she ordered.

Clint was gone in a flash, and someone brought over a small hand towel, powder blue with frayed edges, and handed it to Frank. He took it easily and folded it up, pressing it against the wound in Mallory's chest.

Frank looked over at Shane as those who remained in the cabin around them wept openly, some of them in a state of half-panic as they talked about fleeing the island, getting the police, or begging Frank to save their friend.

Frank did not speak, he just held Shane's gaze. The look on his face did the job well enough. There was no way he could save Mallory. She was bleeding out, the blood loss was extensive, and the bullet had pierced her lung.

He could do nothing for her.

CHAPTER 9

BLAME GAME

Mallory blinked. There was blood at the corner of her mouth.

"You..." she gasped. The word was a hoarse whisper, and more blood bubbled along her lips, casting them in a frothy crimson. She stared at Shane, and he watched her impassively. He had never enjoyed watching another person die, but he did not think it proper to look away. People deserved to be seen, even people who were fools. Too many people died alone. For better or worse, deserving or not, Mallory would not die alone.

"did... this..."

The bubbles stopped, and her eyes were locked on his, but she no longer saw him. They became unfocused. Shane smiled. In her last breath, she still blamed him for things he hadn't done. If nothing else, the woman was consistent.

"Mallory?" the blonde woman said as Frank sighed, leaning back and taking the pressure off the wound.

"I can't find the..." Clint returned to the door and looked in. "...kit."

Frank was bloody to his wrists. His breath came in misty clouds as the open door flooded the cabin with freezing air. The blonde woman wept loudly. Shane sighed and got to his feet. The man he had knocked out was up and holding a cloth to his bloody nose.

"This is your fault," the man said angrily. Shane laughed.

"My fault? You shot her, Dead Eye," he said.

Anger flashed in the man's eyes, but the effect was less than intimidating with the blood smeared across his face and the cloth on his nose.

"She'd be alive if it weren't for you. None of this would have happened if you weren't here," the man said.

There was muttering among the others, words of agreement. Outside, many of the villagers who had previously gathered to look in had left again. There was yelling in the streets, and bodies rushed by. Many who remained shot Shane looks that ranged from fearful to hateful. They were taking Mallory's opinion to heart. By now, the entire village was aware of what happened. And, from the way things were shaping up, they were hearing that Shane had killed Mallory.

"Sounds like a lot of anger is building out there," Frank said softly.

"Yeah," Shane agreed.

They needed to get out of the cabin. Some of Mallory's supporters were still out and about. They might not have been good shots in a maple forest, but if they were standing in the doorway of a one-room building, Shane's chances of survival would decrease considerably.

Frank got to his feet and made his way to the door with Shane a step behind.

"Where do you think you're going?" the man with the bloody nose demanded.

"Why? Going to stop me?" Shane replied.

He heard Frank next to him drawing in a very quiet sharp breath. He didn't want to antagonize these people any more than they already had been, but Shane had run out of patience. If they wanted to accuse him of murder after they all saw who'd pulled the trigger, he certainly wasn't going to extend any courtesy to them when they questioned him.

The tone of the conversation inside the cabin had become angrier, but no one wanted to make a move. Shane still had his gun, and they were still wrapping their heads around what had happened. Still, if Shane hadn't been armed, he imagined the situation might have gone differently. Or at least they would have tried to make it go differently.

The stragglers backed off outside as Shane and Frank left the building.

Those who had not seen what transpired could now only see Frank covered in blood, and some of it splattered on Shane. They knew Mallory was dead, so it was easy enough to write the rest of the story in their heads based on what they saw.

It took a moment for Shane's eyes to adjust. Even though there was cloud cover and no direct sunlight, the world was almost blindingly white, and he had to squint against the light reflected off the snow all around him. He stood there and watched the others watching him in horror, their feelings painted clearly on their faces.

"I think you guys need to leave again," Clint said.

He was the only person who stayed near them when they left the cabin. The others had all seen what happened. They knew Shane had not shot her, but he had the gun. He had pointed it right on her head. In their minds, Shane was the villain. Never mind what Mallory had done to them, and what she was doing to them. All of that had died with her.

Out on the street, Shane saw Alina. She was near some of the others who were clamoring about and gathering in what looked like the beginning of an angry mob. The population of the village was barely enough to make such a thing a reality, but if they all banded together, they would be a problem.

The young woman looked distressed, her eyes asking questions that she couldn't voice without joining Frank and Shane. It was for the best that she didn't come to them. She didn't need to get caught up in what was about to happen.

Raised voices came to Shane's ear, and he turned to look at the road to the left of Mallory's cabin. A man with a rifle stood in the center of the snowy path. Someone was trying to calm him down, a middle-aged woman that Shane had been introduced to but had never spoken to. She had her hand on his arm as he pulled the trigger. The gun was aimed down, and the bullet embedded itself in a snowy drift a few feet away from Frank.

People screamed in the cabin behind them and on the streets. A second wave of panic erupted. Villagers ran. Some shouted, some called for the shooter to try again, and others simply fled to their homes in fear.

"Yes, Clint, I think you're right," Frank said, ducking out of the way and wiping bloody hands on his pants as he pulled his gloves from his pockets.

The man Shane had punched came for him again, wielding the knife that Mallory had used to cut him. Shane saw him coming from the corner of his eye long before he was within range.

"The hell are you doing, idiot?" Shane grumbled, catching the man by the wrist and punching him in the face a second time. He took the knife this time, throwing it across the road where it disappeared into a snowdrift.

The man hit the ground again, groaning through clenched teeth as a fresh round of blood gushed from his nose and down his chest. Shane had nothing else to say as he left with Frank and Clint, rounding Mallory's cabin to the east between it and the greenhouse, out of the main intersection and away from the people of the village.

"This couldn't have gone worse," Frank said, leading the way.

"They just need to calm down. It was an accident. I saw what happened." Clint looked back as though he thought to return and explain it to people.

"Don't think they want to hear it right now," Shane said.

"No," Clint agreed, "but I can talk to them later. It'll be okay, I think."

"In the meantime," Shane cut him off before he could continue, "where are the boats?"

The three of them had slipped behind the greenhouse, and Frank was making a beeline for the village's eastern border. There was a tangle of old shrubs there, leafless and snow-covered, growing up the side of the hill to the top of the bowl and the way out. He used them to provide stability as he scaled the slippery slope.

"Boats are at the dock," Clint said like it was the most obvious thing in the world. He was climbing the hill with them, and Shane didn't care enough to argue that the man didn't need to come with them, not until they were safely somewhere else.

A second shot cracked the air, and Clint made an audible noise, scrambling up the hill with a new, panicked push of speed.

Shane looked back at the shooter. The man was reloading his weapon. It was Blaine's old Ruger that someone had retrieved from the snow. One shot at a time, but if someone knew what they were doing, it was as deadly as any other weapon.

"The boats are missing." Shane followed the two men up the hill. "We need to find them or another radio. Did Mallory keep a radio?"

"The radios are on the boats." Clint was breathing heavily as he scaled the hill. He was not used to being shot at and was holding his fear in check. Shane assumed the man regretted his decision to join them.

They reached the top edge of the bowl, with Frank offering Clint a hand to get up and Shane coming right behind them. They continued east, away from the village and the man coming after them with the rifle.

"You've never seen another radio in town?" Frank asked.

"No, sir," Clint replied. "Never needed them. No one wanted technology."

"What about the boats? Where else can they be docked?" Shane asked.

They were in knee-deep snow, heading toward the eastern wall overlooking the sea. Nothing was in that direction, but it was just to get distance between themselves and the village. They would have to make their way north again in search of more familiar ground. The sugar shack, the forest, even the cave. Some place where they could regroup and consider what would happen next.

The boats had to be somewhere around the shore of the island, but the sheer cliff faces made it almost impossible to see anything unless you were hanging over the edge. If they didn't know where to look, the boats could have been anywhere, and they would have been easily missed.

Three boats meant three people—three captains—knew where they were. Shane was certain that Mallory had not piloted them. So, at least three other people on that island knew where the boats were now. Even if Clint wasn't in the inner circle, there had to be a way to find out.

There was no sign of Hugh outside the village. The ghost would be the best choice when it came to looking for the boats if he was willing to offer his assistance. He didn't need to worry about the height of cliffs or drowning in the ocean by going over the side. He could do a sweep of the island in a fraction of the time that it would take Frank and Shane to search. The question was, could they trust him to do a job like that? And would he be willing to do it?

So far, the ghost of Hugh Carson was not the most amenable spirit Shane had dealt with. He had only bothered to communicate to prevent himself from being destroyed. And now, it seemed he had vanished again.

They at least had an angle to get the ghost on their side in the search for the boats. The sooner they found them, the sooner everyone could leave. That was what Hugh wanted, so it was in his best interest to help. Hopefully, he would see it that way as well.

Frank turned to the north after passing behind a small copse of trees that offered cover from anyone observing back at the village, stopping to gather the other two men.

"Clint, I think you need to go back to town," he said. "You don't want them thinking you've joined us and are against them, or anything."

"I'm not against anyone," the other man assured him. Frank smiled and patted him on the shoulder.

"I know you're not. But I don't want *them* to think it. You should go home. It'll be safer."

Clint did not need to be talked into it. He was scared and unsure of what to do, likely as a result of Mallory's death.

"I will, Frank. I'll tell them you guys didn't do this, either. It was an accident. Everyone saw it."

"Thank you," Frank said. "Do that. Get them to listen. Get them to realize they need to leave this place. Even without Mallory, everyone is still in danger."

"Okay, I will. I promise." Clint looked at them awkwardly for a moment and then nodded, offering a half wave. "I'm going now."

"Take care of yourself. We'll find you again later. Remember, find out about radios and the boats, if you can," Shane said.

"I will, Shane." Clint nodded and then headed back the way they had come.

Shane and Frank waited only a moment before starting north again. The sugar shack was the closest destination. If nothing else, it offered warmth and a place to plan their next move.

CHAPTER 10

THE LOYALIST

They had stopped next to an overgrown Rose of Sharon bush; its withered pink flowers still attached to some of the branches. It provided minimal cover as the men crouched down and watched the sugar shack in the distance. Smoke rose from the chimney, thick and puffy gray. A man with a rifle was pacing the western face of the building, mostly just in a small, lazy circle, and then retracing his footsteps.

"That's one of Blaine's men," Shane said.

He recognized the man, even at a distance. He had backed Blaine up in the village, and he had been in one of the groups that had searched the forest. Clint had told them that some of the people who had gone out the night before had not come back. They must have all held up in the sugar shack. There was no telling how many were inside, but at least nine men went into the woods looking for them. Three were dead now that Shane knew of, including Blaine. So, possibly six of them were waiting in the shack.

They must have gotten word that they needed to wait in the shack and who knows what else. But if they were waiting for Blaine or Mallory, they would be sorely disappointed.

If anyone was likely to know where the boats were, Shane assumed it was this crew. If none of them moved the boats directly, they were in close contact with the people who would have been responsible. There was some potential for information to be gleaned from taking the risk of approaching the shack.

"We don't have to go there. We could head back to the cave," Frank suggested.

"We could," Shane agreed, "but no one in the cave has seen a boat."

Frank nodded, and they continued to observe the shack. If the man outside was a guard, he was doing a poor job. His only movement seemed to be for the sake of not letting his feet freeze. He was not covering the back of the building or the sides. It would be easy enough to sneak up on him. There were no windows on the far side of the shack, so no one would see them coming.

"They're likely all armed," Frank pointed out.

"They're terrible shots," Shane countered.

"Only need to get lucky once."

"You voting no?" Shane asked.

Frank looked at him and then back at the sugar shack and the ineffectual guard out front. He was silent for a long moment and then finally shook his head.

"No, you're right. This is probably our best chance."

They continued to watch the guard to see if he would change his pattern. Aside from shifting from foot to foot, obviously cold and wanting to be somewhere else, he did nothing.

"We head 'round the back, draw him in?" Frank suggested.

"Yeah," Shane agreed.

Shane took the lead, staying low, and using shrubs and snow drifts as cover. The deep snow made it easy to stay out of sight, not that there was much risk of being noticed by the guard. They circled wide of the sugar shack until they were behind the eastern wall. From that side, it was only timber; no doors or windows had been cut into it. They were able to sneak up quickly to the edge of the wall.

Frank waited as Shane pressed his ear to the wood, closed his eyes, and concentrated. The timber was thick but not fully insulating. He heard voices inside, though it was impossible to make out the words. The sound was muffled, and he could only make out differences in tone to identify different speakers. At least three distinct voices. Their guess of six was still on the table.

He pulled away from the wall and made his way to the southeast corner, peering around the side. The guard was not visible from that position; he had taken up a more central stance to loiter, nearly directly in front of the shack. It allowed Shane and Frank to creep around the building's southern wall.

At the closer distance, they heard the man with the rifle grumbling to himself. Some of it was too quiet, but Shane picked out the occasional curse word. It sounded like he was unhappy with the duties he had been given and was venting his frustrations. It meant he was likely not paying close attention to what was happening around him. It would not be too hard to distract him.

Shane nodded to Frank, and the other man slipped back the way they had come. He paused a beat, looking at the guard before emitting a series of quick whistles, mimicking the cry of a bird.

Nothing happened. He waited with his back pressed against the wall and then whistled again. The guard stopped talking, and Shane heard snow crunching. He followed Frank's tracks around the side of the sugar shack and then continued to the east. Frank waited at the wall, several paces behind, as Shane put three yards of distance between himself and the corner of the building and then ducked behind the snow drift.

The guard came around the side of the building.

"Hello?" he said, seeing the tracks in the snow.

Shane heard him pull back the bolt on the rifle as the soft crunch of boots in snow got closer. A smart man would have alerted the people inside that something was going on. A smarter man would not have walked blindly around the corner of a building without having his weapon ready.

After counting the footsteps to gauge the distance, Shane stood slowly with his hands in the air.

"Hold it right there," the man said, as though he had caught Shane, rather than Shane simply standing in front of him. The guard was one pace from the rear corner of the sugar shack. He took that one last step with the barrel of his gun trained on Shane.

Frank was fast. One hand had the barrel of the gun raised, and with the other arm, he drove an elbow strike into the side of the guard's head. The man crumbled quickly, and Shane joined Frank as they subdued him and rolled him over.

"You learning Muay Thai?" Shane asked as Frank held the guard down, pulling the man's scarf over his mouth to muffle any noise.

"Krav Maga." Frank smiled. "Former client has a school in Vermont, offered me some lessons."

"The hell have I been doing all the fighting for?"

"You've been fighting the dead," Frank pointed out.

They secured the scarf around the man's mouth and used the long, loose ends to tie his wrists behind his back. Shane took one ankle, and Frank took the other, and they swiftly dragged the man away from the sugar shack, well out of earshot, taking him behind some of the scrub bushes a short distance to the east, closer to the ocean.

When they were securely away from the others, they dropped the man and pulled the gag off his mouth.

"You're going to pay for this," the man said.

"Really? How?" Shane asked.

The question seemed to briefly stump the guard.

"When Blaine—"

"Blaine's dead. Try again."

"What?"

The man was shocked. His anger was quickly replaced by fear, and then that washed away to be replaced with anger once more.

"You're lying," the guard said with all the confidence a man who had no idea what he was talking about could muster. "Mallory will—"

"Sorry, bud, that's two dead. Who's your number three?"

The guard shook his head.

"Mallory is not dead."

"Just died." Frank held up his hands, removing a glove. Blood was still caked around his nails and between his fingers, dried to an almost brown color and flaking away as he flexed his hand.

"Shot," Shane added. "Which means both of your bosses… or leaders… or whoever you feel like they were are gone. There's no one here to tell you what to do anymore."

"I don't believe you," the guard said.

Shane shrugged.

"I don't care."

"This island is not safe. You know that. Whether you think we're the problem or something else, you know we need to get away from here." Frank tried a different tactic.

"You just want to get back to the mainland. Bring the cops here. You'll ruin this place."

"Buddy, it's about as ruined as a place can get. You'll all be dead by Saturday at the rate people drop around here," Shane told him.

"Even with Mallory gone, people are going to die. These aren't sacrifices for some nature spirit," Frank said.

The guard looked at him, his eyes wide with a sort of perplexed wonder, and then he started laughing. Shane raised an eyebrow and Frank frowned.

"Are you stupid?" He looked from Frank to Shane and back. "Do you think we're all children here? Dumb hippies with our heads in our asses?"

"That a trick question?" Shane asked, netting an aggravated glance from Frank.

"I got twenty-five years waiting for me if I go back to Maine. At least. They got me on an armed robbery and drug charges, plus a parole violation, and God knows what else. You think I care who dies on this rock or why? I've been here for six years. All the food I can eat, my own place, friends, comic books, and places to fish. This is paradise to me."

Shane chuckled softly, angering the man in the process.

"You think I'm joking, tough guy?"

"No, it's just funny, I don't know how you committed armed robbery when you couldn't shoot the broad side of a barn."

The man's jaw clenched, and he balled his hands into fists.

"I had a knife," he said, and Shane laughed out loud.

"You are some kind of loser, huh? Ended up on cannibal murderer island, and you still think you're ahead of the game. Amazing."

"Shane…" Frank said.

"Yeah. Anyway." Shane nodded to his friend. He knew Frank needed him to dial it down. They were looking for information.

"It was worth it for you on this island for six years," Frank said to the restrained man. "I understand that. But things are different now. Mallory is dead. Blaine was taken in the night, along with Miriam. Two more of you died pursuing us; two others were taken into the woods by the ghosts that reside there. That's at least seven that I know of in one day. One day!"

He spoke with an urgency to get the point across to the man. There was no point in staying any longer. They would not survive. No one would.

The man laughed again.

"You think I'm gonna believe anything you say? Mallory's not dead; she never even leaves the village. Blaine made it back last night. I saw him go myself. He left us here to watch this place for you two. You guys are the ones who are dead, you just don't know it yet."

Frank sighed, and Shane considered gagging the man again.

"Think the cold froze his brain," Shane said.

"I can't make you believe us if you don't want to. You'll learn the truth in time. But I'm going to need you to tell us where the boats are," Frank said.

"I'm not going to tell you a goddamn thing," the guard spat.

Shane laughed again, and the man sneered at him.

"What the hell is so funny this time?"

"Now I get to make you tell me," Shane answered.

Chapter 11
The Feasting Hour

Clint was flustered. He had never been good at getting people to listen to him. He never felt like people heard him or cared about what he had to say, but that was mostly okay. He had a home and people who at least liked him, he had a job, and things were good. Until they weren't.

After his parents died, he couldn't stay in the house anymore. His job at the grocery store didn't pay enough, so the bank took the house. He got a little apartment, but it was very hard, and sometimes he missed bills, and eventually, the landlord kicked him out because he forgot to pay for his electricity.

For a while, he rented a room in an old lady's house. And then he was homeless. Sometimes he could get day-to-day work doing odd jobs, but it was hard, and it didn't give him a lot of money. Sometimes, at the end of the day while he was waiting for a ride from a construction site or a farm, he would get robbed, and they would take all the money he'd made.

One day, he heard about a place where they would give you a home and food. They would even give you a job, and all you had to do was just be there. It sounded great to him, so when the boat came in from Maple Grove, he was on it. He had lived in the little village ever since.

That was three years ago.

In some ways, he considered the people of the village his family. He knew each of them very well, but he also knew people did not take him seriously. Clint had never been a smart man, but he was smart enough to know that he wasn't smart. He knew that people didn't think he was important or that he had good ideas. They would tell him to do things, but they didn't listen when he had things to say. And that was a real problem now.

Everyone knew what had happened to Mallory. They had put her body in the greenhouse, on one of the empty tables. It would stay cold there, and they could figure out what to do with her. She couldn't be buried yet because the ground was frozen.

"It wasn't Shane." Clint interrupted a conversation in the Great Hall between Luke and Helen and some others. Everyone was spreading the rumor, even people who knew that Gareth pulled the trigger.

Most everyone ignored Clint when he said that. If they heard him, they just told him to stop talking. It was like nobody cared about the truth. Nobody cared what was going on. That was very frustrating.

The remaining village elders were meeting in the Great Hall to discuss what should happen next. Mallory had always had the final word, but she usually asked the elders what they thought, and oftentimes, they had a vote. But without Mallory, no one knew who was in charge and who should have the final word.

Some people wanted to go back to the mainland. They believed Shane and Frank that the island would get worse and that they all needed to go. But only a few people thought that way. Most of them wanted to go to the mainland to get the police so Shane could be punished for what had happened. Others didn't want to do anything except what Mallory had done. They wanted to take care of things themselves, and that meant they wanted to kill Frank and Shane.

Clint did not know which side would win the argument. A lot of people were yelling, and a lot of people were upset. But the number of people who wanted to listen to Frank and Shane was very small, and that worried Clint.

He wished things could have stayed simple. He liked it best when everyone was just happy all the time. Maybe that was wrong. Now that he knew what Mallory was doing, and that the people who disappeared once or twice a year didn't really leave the island, he knew things weren't as good as he thought they had been. Mallory had lied to him, and that was wrong. But he still felt like there were good times, and everyone else was happy.

"This is a matter for the police." Helen raised her voice. "How many more people need to die before we accept that we can't handle this on our own?"

"This isn't even *our* island." Luke drowned her out. He stood and looked around the room. Luke was very old but very intense, and he made Clint uncomfortable.

"Do you people not understand that? Do you think Mallory had a deed to this place? This is the property of the state of Maine. The government owns this island. We're squatters at best. If we let the police come here, if they look too closely at us, then what? We get evicted. When's the last time any of you paid taxes? Paid your debts from before? This is our problem to deal with. It has to be."

Other people looked concerned. Luke always made good points. People were likely to listen to him because of it, even though Clint did not think his point was that good. He wasn't sure that paying taxes and being killed by a ghost were equal concerns.

He tried to think of some way to get people to listen, to understand how serious everything was, but a sound from outside distracted him. Glass was breaking, a lot of it from the sound of things. Most of the cabins in town only had one or two small windows. But the greenhouse was almost all glass.

Clint was the first one to the door. Others in the hall had heard it, and they followed him as he headed out into the cold, doing up his jacket as he went. The greenhouse was only a few yards away. People didn't go in there very often in the winter. And certainly, no one would break anything there unless it was by accident. What Clint saw when he got outside did not look like an accident.

The front of the greenhouse had been smashed in. The door and the surrounding windows were broken, and fragments of glass were scattered about in the snow. He approached it more with curiosity than caution because he didn't understand what could have done such damage. It looked like someone had crashed something into it, but there were no tracks in the snow except for the tracks of those who had taken Mallory's body there earlier. Nothing was broken when they left.

Noises came from within the greenhouse. Clint walked slowly, leaning forward, and craning his neck to see what was there. Once he saw what had broken into the building, he froze.

There were two of them, one on either side of Mallory's body. Their backs were to Clint, what remained of them at least, and they were making soft, wet noises. Intermittently, one or the other released a quiet moan like a satisfied sound that made Clint grimace.

He had seen the monster that had come into the village last night. Ghost, Shane had called it. Only now, there were two of them. Each one was missing flesh across its body. It looked as though someone had peeled the back off the one on the left, right down to the ribs. Their arms were barely more than bone. The one on the right had more wet-looking bits of flesh hanging from its shoulders.

With their heads down, it was hard for Clint to understand what they were doing at first. Part of him understood, but he couldn't accept what he saw. He knew they were eating her, but it didn't make sense that such a thing would be happening.

Every few moments, something soft plopped to the ground, hitting the plywood floor of the greenhouse with a soft, squishing sound. Clint stared at the ground beneath the feet of the ghost on the left. A small, sloppy pile of red and pink slime was building up. Another chunk plopped to the floor. It was meat. He was looking at a pile of chewed-up meat.

Whatever they were taking from Mallory, they were chewing it, and swallowing it, but it fell through their bodies as though they had holes in their guts. The meat fell, and they continued eating like nothing out of the ordinary was happening.

Someone behind Clint screamed, and the ghost on the left stood up straight and turned its head. Clint felt his muscles stiffen, like the freezing winter had suddenly invaded every bit of his insides.

The creature had no lips, no nose, and no eyes. Its face had been torn away. Two, empty black caverns met his gaze and even though there were no eyes there, Clint knew it was looking at him. He felt it. He knew it saw him as clearly as he saw it.

"Oh…"

He didn't know what he wanted to say; it was the only word that could come out of his mouth. Somewhere in his mind, he wanted to scream. Or maybe tell everyone to run away. Another part of him wanted to rush into the greenhouse and save Mallory, even though she was already dead. He would fight off those monsters and send them back to the forest, scaring them so badly that they would never come back. But all of that was deep, deep in his mind, buried behind the fear that kept him frozen and silent.

The ghost flexed its jaws. Its teeth chattered a quick percussive movement, six or seven clicks in a row. Clint didn't know if it meant something like a threat or laughter. But instead of coming for him or rushing after the people on the streets as they screamed and ran, leaving Clint behind, the ghost just turned and kept eating through Mallory's neck and shoulder.

Behind Clint, back at the Great Hall, the screaming changed. There was a squelching sound, and it triggered something in Clint's mind. His body released him, his instinct to flee was finally unburdened, and he knew he should run. But something was happening behind him. Something had changed.

He turned in the snow, ready to head back, and watched a third ghost lift Luke's body from the snow. The older man's throat had been torn out. A swath of the trampled, white path was now stained crimson.

Steam rose from the wound in the old man's throat. The new ghost tossed the old man over its shoulder, and Clint saw that he was still alive and gasping his final breaths. They made eye contact as blood ran down Luke's face in a sheet, his head upside-down as the ghost carried him away.

Luke sputtered, gurgling something. Clint couldn't tell if he was speaking or if it was just the final breath escaping his body. A moment later, there was no more sound, but his eyes remained open as blood flowed across them, obscuring them and then dripping from his forehead. He left a trail in the snow while the ghost wandered out of the town as though it had all the time in the world.

Clint watched the ghost leave, looking at the old man's blood-stained body hanging over its back. The two in the greenhouse snapped at each other, the sound of their teeth chattering back and forth grating in his ears. Finally, the faceless one on the left sunk a hand into the wounds it had opened in Mallory's chest and dragged her out of the greenhouse.

The other ghost followed, scuttling on all fours like a dog, following the body its companion was dragging. It tried to pull Mallory away, but the first ghost would not allow it.

Frustrated, the second ghost looked around. This one still had eyes, and it glanced at Clint. For a moment, he feared that it would come for him, but the ghost turned his head sharply and then darted down the pathway next to the Great Hall.

Another scream pierced the silence, and the ghost returned, dragging Helen with it.

"No…" Clint said softly. Helen was a nice lady, she reminded him of his Aunt Patricia.

He didn't know what to do. He didn't know how to fight a ghost, but he didn't want to see Helen die as Luke had just died. Clint ran after them, even as the ghost was dragging her after the other two. The ghost had her by the hair, dragging her across the ground as it scrambled toward the hill that led up and out of town.

Clint caught up with them and grabbed Helen's hand. He tried to pull her away but as soon as it felt resistance, the ghost turned its head. It snarled at Clint, its mouth a shredded mess of wounded flesh and bite marks. With its free hand, the ghost backhanded him so hard that it knocked him off his feet.

Clint landed in the snow with a cry of pain. It felt like someone had swung a baseball bat into his chest.

Everyone in the village had fled to their homes, hiding from the horror they had just witnessed. Everyone had left Clint alone in the street to witness the ghosts carrying two more people from the village. He alone listened to Helen's screams.

Clint sat up as the ghost crested the ridge at the northern edge of town, dragging the screaming woman away. He breathed heavily, gasping to catch his breath. He could do nothing to save her, but her screams continued. Everyone must have heard them, but no one came outside.

He hadn't wanted to believe Shane and Frank when they said what was happening. He trusted them, but he didn't want to believe them. He knew most of the people in the village didn't want to believe them, either. But now they would have to see the truth.

No one was safe, and they would all be dead in a matter of days if they didn't do something.

CHAPTER 12

DENIED

Shane sat back on his haunches and sighed. The guard, whose name was Lonnie, knew nothing. No one trusted him with any information. At the threat of several broken fingers, his lips loosened considerably, and his attitude changed to become helpful. The problem was that all his information was useless.

Five other people were in the sugar shack. Blaine had told them to stay there and watch for Shane and Frank, but that had been the night before. They had already failed in their mission once, and they would have failed again if Shane and Frank hadn't stopped of their own accord. They had three guns among them, and Lonnie was chosen as the guard because he was the only person in the group who had ever shot a gun. When pressed to explain his experience, Lonnie said he used to target shoot with his dad as a kid. He hadn't held a rifle in more than thirty years.

"I feel like we're almost taking advantage of these people," Shane said. "I should be embarrassed fighting guys like this."

"One's history of and skill at violence don't take away their willingness to cause harm," Frank pointed out. "These men tried to kill us. More than once."

"You can build a bridge out of cardboard boxes and banana peels, too. Doesn't mean anyone needs to take it seriously."

Frank raised an eyebrow and, though he was trying to stay serious, had to suppress a laugh.

"That's not a saying, is it?"

"No," Shane admitted. "But you have to admit…"

"I understand," Frank agreed.

Lonnie did not know where the boats had been moved to. He was aware that Mallory had sent people to move them, but it was nothing he was involved with. Only the pilots of the boats knew where they were.

"Who piloted the boats?" Shane asked.

"Probably Grady, Stew, and Luis."

Shane remained silent, waiting for a follow-up. When none came, he suppressed a sigh.

"Who are Grady, Stew, and Luis, and where do we find them?"

"They're just guys. In the village. Everyone's in the village," Lonnie said.

Shane felt like he needed to threaten to break another finger if he wanted to get Lonnie's head in the game and give some useful answers. Instead, a sound from farther to the West drew his attention away.

Someone was screaming. They were well past the sugar shack, but the still, cold air allowed sound to travel across the empty field.

"You hear that?" Shane asked Frank.

Frank held still and listened. Lonnie began to speak, and Shane pressed a hand over the man's mouth. The sound returned, shrill, and panicked. A woman was screaming.

"In the field. Has to be a villager," Frank said.

"They took someone," Shane said.

They left Lonnie where he was, bound with his scarf, and ran toward the sugar shack. No one inside the building had come out. Either they hadn't heard the screaming, or they didn't care.

Shane and Frank stood at the southern edge of the shack and stared out at the open field where three figures crossed the empty snow plains. The ghost in the lead was carrying a body over its shoulder, but the other two were dragging them. Only one was fighting, at the rear of the pack. They were hard to make out at a distance, but Shane could see a woman struggling to get away from the ghost dragging her toward the forest.

Shane cursed. There was a lot of open space between the sugar shack and the ghosts. Three spirits, and armed men still inside the shack who would be at their backs if they ventured into the open. They were, at the very least, caught between a rock and a hard place. He didn't need to ask Frank what he thought they should do.

Frank was already running. He had stripped off his gloves, exposing the iron rings he wore with their little iron crosses ready to be planted into ghostly flesh. Shane was only a step behind.

Neither man could achieve speed running across the field. The snow was still pristine; no one had ventured out that far. Their saving grace was the fact that dragging a victim meant the ghosts were forced to go slow as well.

The lead ghost carrying a body had gotten far ahead of its peers. The one with the struggling, living victim had fallen far to the back of the pack, and that was where Shane and Frank headed.

Shane felt the burn in his muscles when they were only three-quarters of the way to the ghost. None of the spirits paid him or Frank any mind as they crossed toward the maple forest. They seemed single-minded in their mission, whatever made them want to be in the forest before they finished what they were doing.

The first two ghosts left a trail of blood in the snow, and the third ghost followed through it. Shane couldn't see the other victims, but it was clear they were dead. He wondered if the ghosts were taking the bodies to the circle of graves to feed their brethren. The feasting seemed to be a group activity, though he still couldn't quite understand why.

Shane overtook Frank as they closed the distance between themselves and the screaming woman. Now that he was close enough to see, Shane recognized the woman's face from Mallory's cabin and other places around the village. She seemed to be part of the inner circle. She had been there when Mallory died, but she had not said much.

He guessed the woman to be in her late fifties, short, and frail. The ghost gripped her by the hair, and she held on to it to stop herself from being scalped while simultaneously kicking and digging into the snow. None of her efforts succeeded in slowing the ghost or distracting it.

Shane dropped his gloves and flexed his hands as he ran. He reached the ghost and threw a quick right cross, smashing his fist into the spirit's jaw. The ghost did not expect an attack. He had not even slowed when Shane approached, even though he saw the men coming. With one hand still holding the woman's hair, he hadn't thought to defend himself.

Two teeth flew out of the ghost's lipless mouth. His mangled arms dropped the woman, and Frank was at her side immediately, pulling her away from her attacker and getting her behind him. Shane paid little attention to what they were saying as the ghost rounded on him, its eyes wild with anger and a hint of confusion.

The other two ghosts were farther ahead, still moving, and still distracted. Shane had a short window in which he could do something about this one spirit, and he didn't want to waste it. He gave the ghost no time to adjust to what was happening or figure out what to do. His fists slammed into its face again and again.

With his free hand, Shane grabbed the ghost through a hole in its chest, squeezing a pair of exposed ribs and using them like a handle. A gurgling sound came from the ghost's mouth.

Shane realized as it continued to chatter its teeth that it had no tongue. It looked as though it had been bit off, though there was no way to know if the ghost had done it to himself or if someone had removed the muscle.

One final punch and the ghost's jaw shifted suddenly and harshly to the left. The joints where it was attached to the skull broke, and it hung loose.

"Shane." Frank's tone was sharp with urgency.

"I see," he replied.

The ghosts in the distance had realized what was happening. Both had dropped the bodies they carried and were bounding back toward Shane like animals running through the snow. Frank was quick to put himself between Shane and the new ghosts, but Shane realized his chances against two, even with iron rings, were dangerously slim.

The ghost he held reached for his throat. Cold, fleshless fingers clawed at his neck. Shane drew the ghost closer, letting it get a grip but at the same time getting his hands on its head.

He gripped the ghost tightly, driving his thumbs into the freezing, gelatinous eye sockets as he pushed his hands together. The ghost released him quickly, struggling in his grip and pulling his hands away as Shane forced its body to the ground, pushing its head into the snow. The other two spirits were almost upon Frank, and Shane put his body weight behind his assault.

With a crisp snapping sound, the ghost's skull finally cracked. It released a strained gurgle and then its head imploded, crushing under Shane's weight. An instant later, the ghost came apart, exploding outward and knocking Shane back into the snow at Frank's feet.

The force didn't quite knock the wind out of him, but he gasped in a deep breath and struggled back to his feet in time to see Frank's fist pummel the first of the ghosts square in the forehead.

One punch was all that was needed. The iron of the ring did its work, and the ghost vanished, banished to wherever its haunted item waited. The second ghost was nimbler, and dodged Frank's attack.

Shane was on his feet again as the ghost made a play for Frank, slashing toward him with its ragged, bony, clawlike fingers. Shane moved in as Frank took a step back, catching the ghost's wrist and pulling it forward.

The movement was swift and fluid. Frank pivoted as Shane stepped back, dragging the ghost with him. The ring on Frank's finger hit the back of the ghost's head on the way down and before the spirit even fell into the snow where Shane had been leading it, it was gone.

"You have to go," Frank said to the woman they had rescued. She had not gotten to her feet yet; she was still sobbing in the snow. Her scalp was bleeding where the ghost had pulled chunks of hair loose, but she would survive. As long as she got away, she would survive.

"They're coming back," Shane said to her, joining Frank, and lifting the woman by her arm. "Get home and get safe."

"Please," the woman said. "Don't make me go back alone."

She clutched at Frank and Shane, looking to either of them for salvation.

"You can make it on your own," Frank assured her. "It will be fine."

As if to mock Frank's words, a keening howl arose from within the forest. It was not a bestial cry; there was no mistaking it for an animal. But it hardly sounded like the sound a man would make, either. It was something wholly unique, the product of the ruined physiology of a dead man back from the grave. It warbled and echoed across the snow.

A ghost broke free from the tree line, running toward the two men, and a second joined. Only a few steps behind, a third and fourth appeared, and finally, the fifth ghost. They ran together like a pack, only one of them upright on two legs while the others used their hands and ran in a crouch, loping like animals.

"Run now!" Shane yelled at the woman from the village.

He hoped she knew she needed to save herself.

CHAPTER 13

DEAD OR DEAD

The woman froze, and Shane cursed loudly. He had no time to deal with her any longer or worry about what she was doing. It was too late for her to escape. The ghosts would be on her within seconds if she tried. She would have to stay where she was, and he would do his best to keep her safe.

The distance between them and the ghosts was still substantial, but the spirits were not slowed by the snow. There was nowhere for Shane, Frank, and the woman to go. Even the sugar shack would be too far away for them to make it. Not that it would have offered them cover.

Shane slipped an iron ring over the fingers on each hand and then balled them into fists, raising his arms in expectation of what was to come. Fighting all five was a losing prospect if he was fighting to win. They would come too fast and too hard to handle together. He and Frank would have to work at tiring them out.

Their haunted items were not far away, but being sent back several times in a row might give them pause to think of what they were doing. Time was all Shane needed. Time and space. If he could get them alone, one at a time, if he could have one long enough to put an end to it, he could take them all out. But there were a lot of ifs in that equation.

"Nothing fancy," Shane said.

"I'm not much for fancy," Frank agreed.

The men stood shoulder to shoulder with only a slight gap between them to allow them to move without running into each other. The woman from the village was behind them, holding herself and sobbing loudly.

They didn't make much of a break wall to keep the ghosts at bay, but it would have to do.

The first of the ghosts closed in, and as Shane prepared for the attack, a gunshot rang out. He heard the round zip by his head. It had missed him by a decent margin, but it was closer than it needed to be.

"Lonnie," Frank said.

The man had somehow gotten free and was standing in front of the shack with the rifle in his hands. The others from the shack had filtered out, shouting orders at one another as a second shot was fired by another gunman.

Shane swore again, wishing he had broken Lonnie's fingers so he couldn't handle the gun. There was no time to worry about it, though. He needed to focus on the greater danger.

The first ghost jumped, leaping toward Frank with its arms outstretched. Shane crouched and raised his hand in an uppercut, taking the ghost with a shot to the chest before its hands got close to Frank. It vanished, but the second ghost was already there, and the third was only a step behind.

Frank took one out while Shane took longer with the third as it avoided his swings. It was the first one he had vanished, now more cautious about what it did.

Two more gunshots whizzed by, one of them close enough that it caused the snow in front of Shane to explode in a tiny puff of white when it hit the ground.

Frank was tangling with the fourth ghost, looking to make contact, but it was dodging too, taking swipes with its ragged hands and then backing away before he could counter.

The village elder screamed, and Shane realized the fifth ghost had circled them. Shane kicked at the knee of the ghost he was tangling with and knocked it to the ground, leaving it before turning to throw a punch at the ghost coming for the woman.

The iron did its job, and the ghost vanished. Cold hands grasped his back, and the ghost he had briefly debilitated was back on him, digging claws into his shoulders through his coat. The thickness of the garment prevented them from going too deep, but he could feel them just piercing his skin. He growled between clenched teeth as the thing dragged him to the ground.

A second later, the ghost was gone, and Frank was there, offering Shane a hand up. The first ghost had already returned. They had fallen into a routine now. In the time it took them to eliminate all five, the first was back. Shane was hoping for a bigger gap, but he would have to make do.

The gunmen had fallen into their own routine as well. Loading, firing, reloading. Their aim was not improving, but Frank was right. One lucky shot was all they needed.

Shane met the attacking ghost and, as with the others, this one had learned. It avoided his attacks, outmaneuvering him while not being touched by the iron rings. They sparred, and the ghost kept its distance long enough to allow its companions to return. Five spirits surrounded Shane, Frank, and the woman from the village.

The ghosts spread out, most of them staying close to the ground, and keeping at enough of a distance that they could not be hit by a surprise strike. More shots rang out and Shane swore again as he took a swing at one of the spirits that moved in on him.

The ghosts attacked as one. All five moved in at different points. Two of them set their sights on Shane, one going high on the body and one going low. They might have seemed like animals, but their attack was well-coordinated this time. With no communication between them, it seemed to be either something they had done in the past or impressive instincts at play.

Frank was taken to the ground and screamed as one of them bit his leg, finding purchase even through his jeans. Shane was pulled to the ground as well, and the sound of the woman from the village screaming pierced the relative silence of the field. The final ghost had gone for her. She was defenseless and unable to do anything as it dragged her away from the group and swiftly dove at her throat.

Shane fought off one of the ghosts, kicking out to get the second away and then backhanding the first to allow his iron ring to make contact with the ghost's face. He was too slow and too clumsy getting away from them in the snow, though. Before he even got to his feet to go after the woman, her throat had been torn open. Blood gushed out, bathing Shane and the surrounding area with a forceful spray before it lessened to a trickle.

Frank cried out, knocking away his attackers as well. His voice was full of anguish at the sight of the woman he barely knew dying before their eyes. He had only wanted to help these people, and they were fighting him tooth and claw over it.

A bullet hit the ground next to Shane's head. He rolled over in the snow and struck out at the last ghost attacking him, then got to his feet. Pulling the iron rings from his fingers, he covered the distance between himself and the ghost chewing on the dead woman's face and neck in seconds.

The woman's body fell as Shane dragged the ghost down to the snow. He caught it by surprise, lost in the act of feeding on the woman. It had not seen Shane coming and did nothing to protect itself. Once he had it on the ground, his attack was messy but brutal. He planted a knee against the ghost's shoulder and quickly overextended and broke the arm. The fractured bone pulled away, and he threw it aside like garbage.

"Shane," Frank called out.

The other spirits were returning. They were bounding across the field, and Shane only had seconds to spare. With a knee planted firmly in the ghost's spine, he wrenched its head to one side and then strained his body, pulling the skull away and crushing it as it broke free.

The release of energy knocked Shane back, and in the same instant, a round from one of the rifles passed through the air where he had been seconds earlier. He heard one of the gunmen curse, the sound barely reaching his ear. It was the best shot they had taken so far, and it would have killed him had he not moved.

"We have to get out of here," Shane said.

Two more gunshots rang out, these missing by a wider margin. Frank looked back at the dead woman in the snow, and Shane kept his focus on the ghosts.

"There's nowhere to go," Frank pointed out.

"The woods," Shane said.

Frank looked at him like he might have lost his mind.

"We're fighting them, anyway. At least there we won't get shot as easily."

Any choice was a terrible choice, but at least with the cover of the trees, the villagers at the sugar shack were less likely to get even a lucky shot. And if they dared to follow them, the ghosts would likely make quick work of them. It was trading two problems for one problem, and in Shane's mind, that was a good deal.

"This has gotten out of control." Frank looked at the dead woman in the snow.

"Tell me about it… later," Shane replied.

He started moving then, legs pumping as he ran to meet the ghosts as best he could in the deep snow. Frank joined him, and they cut the distance between themselves and their attackers by a few yards before they met. The ghosts were so fast in the snow, unencumbered and unfazed by it.

The shooters reset to adjust their aim. Shane met the first ghost by collapsing to his knees and punching it in the gut. It was gone in an instant. As the second dove to attack him, an uppercut to the jaw took it out as well. He was removing the third as Frank took out the fourth and then they continued trudging through snow, closing the gap between themselves and the forest.

Lonnie shouted something from the shack. Shane couldn't make it out, but it sounded like an insult. He was trying to get the others to join him, to leave the safety of the shack, and follow Shane and Frank to the woods. It didn't look like he was having much luck.

Shane and Frank were close to the tree line when the four ghosts returned. A bullet hit a tree several yards from Shane. The ghosts were not so quick to attack this time; they approached and circled again. They spread out, looking to surround the two men, but Shane did not have the patience to play it out. He took on the first one, rushing it and banishing it back to its haunted item with an inelegant backhand slap.

He started forward again with Frank at his side. They forced the ghosts to either follow back to the woods or be left behind. Frank handled the second one, and by the time the third attacked Shane, they were in the tree line, barely protected by the first several scattered tree trunks.

Only the fourth remained when the shooting stopped. Lonnie and the others realized they were out of luck, that shooting through the trees was a fruitless exercise.

The snow was shallower and easier to maneuver in between the more densely packed trees, and Shane was finally able to get some speed with his footing. When the fourth ghost attacked, he grabbed it by the throat and before he could cause any serious damage, the ring met with ragged flesh, and that ghost was gone as well.

They continued deeper into the maple forest, past the aluminum buckets of sap, and into the denser growth.

"They're gone," Frank said, after only a couple of minutes of travel.

The ghosts had not returned for another round once the men entered the forest. In fact, they were nowhere to be seen.

"Not gone," Shane said. "Planning something."

CHAPTER 14
THE HERDING

The forest was a maze of footprints. It was the first time since Frank and Shane had arrived at Maple Grove that Shane had seen tracks, and they were in abundance. There was no way they were left by the villagers in the sugar shack. Blaine and his men had been out in the woods the day before, but the blizzard would have covered up anything they left. The tracks were made by the ghosts. They were intentional, and they were there to send a message.

The woods were not safe, and they were not alone.

They needed to put some distance between themselves and the armed men at the shack. They would be fools to follow, but they *were* fools, so Shane wouldn't be surprised by anything.

There were only four ghosts left. Shane felt like he had a chance of taking out the remaining spirits. It would not be that hard, he just needed to keep them coming as they had been. They needed to keep isolating themselves so he could get them one at a time.

The problem with Shane's plan was that the ghosts were not cooperating. They did not think like men thought anymore, but they were also not purely beasts. They were intelligent enough to learn. They had changed their strategy in the field to survive. Now they had adapted again.

Despite the seemingly infinite barrage of tracks that crisscrossed the snow, there was no sign of anyone who had made them. The ghosts were hidden, biding their time.

Shane and Frank continued deeper into the forest, putting as much tree cover between themselves and the villagers as they could. They had no specific destination in mind. The cave was the only place they knew of where they could rest or take cover, but there was no point in going there. They needed to find the boats. They needed to find a radio. There had to be a way to find what they were looking for while avoiding another assault from the people of the island or the ghosts.

Shane slowed his pace after several minutes, and Frank joined him. He was scanning the forest in every direction, occasionally doing a full turn to look behind them to see if they had a tail. Eventually, he noticed something about the surrounding woods. More specifically, it was what he didn't notice that drew his attention.

"Do you recognize any of this?" he asked.

Frank paused long enough to do a full turn, getting his bearings as best he could.

"No," he said finally.

Shane grunted. They had not been on the island for a very long time, and a forest in the snow was not the easiest landscape to learn. That said, he had come to recognize some specific features. There had always been a rise to the north, and another to the west. There was the ring of stones, and the ravine where Frank had found the bodies. The little stream Shane had fallen into. They should have seen some of that by now, as far into the woods as they had traveled.

"The buckets are gone," Frank pointed out after a moment.

Shane had not even noticed that; he was too busy looking for landmarks. There were no aluminum buckets attached to any of the trees. That happened deeper in the forest. Much deeper. Or at least that was how it had been.

They were in a part of the woods they had never been in, even though they should not have been. Within the trees, given the time of day, Shane was not even sure which direction they were facing. The overcast sky made it hard to navigate. They should have been traveling north, but it was impossible to tell.

Their tracks were also gone, buried under the hundreds of others that went in every direction. It meant there was no way to tell if they had been traveling in a straight line or somehow walking in circles.

"Is this a trick?" Frank asked.

"Getting here was," Shane said. "I don't think this is an illusion. But how we got here? Can't say."

Some ghosts were highly skilled at crafting illusions, making a person see what they wanted them to see. They could be intensely real. But a crafty ghost could use illusion to trick you in other ways. Like making you think you were walking in one direction when you were walking in another.

The men had been in a rush, just heading forward to get away from Lonnie and the other gunmen. It gave the spirits of the woods a good opportunity to prey on the fact that neither Shane nor Frank was headed in a specific direction. They had no goal in mind. Their wish had essentially been fulfilled. They had gone somewhere, they just didn't know *where*.

Shane got a sense of at least where they were relative to the island. They had to be closer to one side than the other. The eastern wall or the western wall. He listened for the sounds of the ocean, and the waves crashing against the rocks. Instead, all he heard was the emptiness of the woods and the lack of sound. The way a vast, open space just sounded in your ears, cavernous and waiting for something to fill it.

"Can you tell where the sun is?" Frank asked.

He was looking up, and he had turned in a full circle more than once. He had walked around several trees and, as Shane looked up, he realized the other man's conundrum. It was not just that the sky was overcast, there was no sense of where behind the clouds the sun might be. It was a uniform white and gray throughout the sky as those fat, slow snowflakes fell. It looked less like the sun was even up there and more like fluorescent lights from a grocery store, just filling the space with a washed-out kind of brightness.

"It's a trap," Shane said.

The reason the ghosts had not come back was that they did not need to come back. Shane and Frank had willingly run into the trap that was left for them. They were stuck somewhere and did not know how to get out. Any method they might have normally used to get out was also not at their disposal.

They could pick a direction. To the left, what should have been west, or to the right, what should have been east. But he knew if they did that, they would not end up where they intended to go. The next step, he assumed, would be to find a way to separate them. It would be easier for the ghosts to handle them one at a time. They were basically turning Shane's plan against him, simple though it was. Isolate and overcome.

"We should keep moving," Shane suggested.

Trap or not, if they stayed put, they were sitting ducks. The cold would eventually get to them, and fighting off attackers with numb hands and feet was not a smart move. If they kept moving, they would at least keep warm.

They continued straight. If the woods were the same as usual, they would have crossed the stream, found the ridge that Shane had been thrown down, and then moved into more unexplored forest ahead. But none of that happened. Nothing was where it was supposed to be.

Minutes passed, and neither man spoke to the other. They were watching the woods, moving not stealthily, because there was no point in hiding, but quickly and cautiously. It was not long before Shane noticed quick, furtive movements around the edges of trees.

He alerted Frank, not with words, but with a simple gesture. The other man nodded. He saw them, too. A shadow here, a glimpse of something barely registered there. The ghosts remained in their peripheral vision, moving among untrampled snowbanks and the thicker trees that hid them.

The farther they traveled, the more frequently Shane noticed them. He wasn't sure if they were trying to remain hidden or just staying out of the way so that any attack on them would fail, as they would be able to escape in time. They made no effort to get closer, however. To Shane, that seemed like herding behavior.

Shane nodded left, and Frank moved with him. They were altering their course to see how their pursuers would alter theirs.

It was not long before the ghosts became more present and aggressive in their actions. They began to slip from behind the trees, no longer running alongside but pursuing. They could have easily overtaken Shane and Frank, but they were not doing so. They were pacing them, herding them again, but more obviously this time.

Only one of them ran like a man, the other three loped like hounds. They moved as a group, the more beastlike ones deferring to the one still on his hind legs. But still, none ventured close.

There was no good opportunity to confront the ghosts. If Shane stopped or turned to take one on, it could have easily vanished among the trees. Or the others could have taken advantage and overwhelmed him. The terrain made it too difficult to gain an upper hand. He would not have enough time to take one out before another one was upon him.

The four had banded too closely together now, anyway. There was no timing gap. If they attacked, they would do it as one. A hit from an iron ring could make them disappear, but by the same token, their ragged, bony fingers only needed one strike somewhere vital. Across the neck, or an artery in the leg or the arm, and either man would be dead in minutes.

"Fight?" Frank asked.

Shane shook his head.

"Not here. That's what they want," he said.

They were running closer now, darting in and out of the trees. Sometimes, they were within just a few inches of Shane or Frank. Had they wanted to, they could have leaped on either man. They weren't ready for a confrontation yet; not one they instigated, anyway. They wanted the living to stop. They wanted them to make a mistake. The ghosts were smarter than they seemed when they were just acting like animals and mindlessly chewing on flesh. They could still strategize.

Shane picked up a sound as they were running. Somewhere ahead of them was the crashing sound of waves against rock. They were coming to one of the shorelines, one of the rock walls that surrounded the island. They would be out of the forest soon enough, but they would also be out of options in terms of where to go.

He was struck suddenly by a story he had heard a long time ago. About a nature film that told the story of lemmings. There was a popular belief for years that lemmings blindly followed one another. To prove this, they were filmed running off a cliff. One of the little animals would go over the edge, and then his companions would follow, an entire pack tumbling to their doom because they couldn't get it in their heads to not run straight into the jaws of death.

The reality was that the lemmings don't do that naturally. Behind the scenes, the men filming the movie scared the animals, herded them toward the edge in such a state of panic that they feared for their lives and the only option was to run off the cliff.

The ghosts were forcing Shane and Frank toward one option. Death.

Unless they figured out a better plan.

CHAPTER 15

THE KING AWOKEN

The sound of crashing waves grew louder. Shane slowed, not wanting to leave the potential cover of the forest just yet. If they were being herded toward a cliff, he didn't want to be exposed. Four ghosts could easily take them over the edge.

If they needed to fight now, Shane decided they would fight now. He stopped, prompting Frank to do the same, and then turned, ready to take on whichever of the ghosts reached him first. Nothing was there.

"I lost them," Frank said.

Shane could not see any of them either. The forest was still and silent, save for the white noise of the waves nearby. Snow still fell in slow, fat, drifting flakes, but there was nothing else to see. All four of the spirits had vanished.

"They wanted us here for something," Frank said softly.

Shane agreed. It was a reasonable assumption, but he couldn't imagine what they would want to do if they weren't there to do it.

"You need to come with me," a voice said suddenly.

Shane was caught off-guard. He didn't like that sensation, and when he turned, Hugh was standing almost right behind him. The ghost could have reached out and put a hand on his shoulder. He had gotten the drop on Shane and Frank with ease.

"Where have you been?"

"Trying to keep you people alive," the ghost answered. "Come. Quickly."

Frank and Shane shared a glance. They would be in no worse position going with Hugh than they would be staying in place. At least it seemed like the ghost was an ally, so that was better than waiting for whatever the other four had planned.

Hugh led them a little farther into the woods, back in the direction Shane suspected was north, until they came across a small clearing in the maple trees where a cluster of moonglow juniper had taken root. The dense evergreens provided some cover as Hugh took them into the center of the growth and then simply crouched down.

"They were going to kill you, you know," Hugh said.

He stared out through the juniper boughs, in the small gap that existed between the trees, watching the woods from which they had just escaped.

"That was the feeling I got, yeah," Shane agreed.

"They vanished. Was that your doing?" Frank asked.

"No," the ghost replied. "Please don't speak."

His tone was almost indifferent, and he had not bothered to look at either man when he spoke. He kept his eyes looking out through the branches of the evergreen, though Shane saw nothing. The trees were too densely packed. They were about six layers deep in them as it was, crowded on all sides by the scratchy, green leaves.

The snow had penetrated the junipers, and the trio was crouched in a bed of dried needles, crunchy and brown on the forest floor beneath them. It was nice to be out of the snow and not feel it underfoot for a change. Their hiding place was well-obscured from the outside world. Someone could be almost on top of them and not see them.

The seconds ticked by into minutes. Two, five, then ten minutes. Shane was patient, waiting for any hint from Hugh about what they were doing, but it soon wore thin.

"Wait," the ghost said, as though sensing Shane's thoughts.

Frank shrugged and remained silent. They continued to wait, and Shane wondered if there was any point to it when, finally, a new sound came to his ear. This was much more distant than the crashing of waves.

From where they were, it seemed back in the direction they had come. Back toward the sugar shack, but not quite. This was still deep in the woods.

"What is that?" Frank whispered.

The sound was deep and resonant. It was somewhere between a howl and a scream. It sounded neither human nor animal, and it was nothing like anything Shane had heard from the ghosts. There was a powerful bass to it. He could feel it in his chest. It reminded him of the calls of male lions, that commanding and impossible-to-ignore sound that couldn't be replicated by human vocal cords.

Shane watched the dried juniper leaves at his feet vibrate. The tiny, brown bundles shook as though the earth was moving underneath him. He could feel it vibrating up through the muscles of his legs, right into the bone.

It was not real. It could not have been. It was a projection of the spirits, an illusion he had never encountered. Making unusual sounds was child's play to a ghost, but this was another level. This was not something he had experienced, and he could not readily explain it.

Why had they gone so far? Why had they chased the two men almost to the cliffs and then retreated deep into the forest to release what had to be meant as an intimidating cry? Shane could not puzzle out what was going on, but it was clear that Hugh had more insight into the issue.

"What's going on?" he asked the ghost.

"You have to stay quiet," the ghost whispered, still not bothering to look at him.

"Whatever that was, it was on the other side of the forest."

"It was not," Hugh said. This time the ghost looked at him, his eyes conveying gravity.

"What—" Shane began.

"You destroyed the other spirits again," Hugh said. "Two, I think. Is that right?"

"Yeah," Shane confirmed in a whisper.

The ghost shook his head. He was missing too much tissue around his mouth to form a proper frown, but Shane thought that was what the ghost was doing.

The sound came again. Shane heard Frank draw in a breath, almost a surprised gasp. He would normally have looked at the other man or maybe even made a joke, but he felt it this time. It was louder now, and his muscles trembled at the sound of it. He felt like he was on a train platform as one rumbled past.

It was as powerful as anything they had ever heard. More than just a freight train, it was like a sustained, focused explosion. It took hold of the maple forest as though holding it in a fist and shaking it violently.

"What are they doing?" Frank asked.

"It's not them," Hugh whispered. "I told you this would happen."

"What would happen?" Shane asked.

"It's like cutting struts on a bridge. One might be fine. Maybe that won't cause a problem. But if you destroy three? That bridge will collapse."

"This is your Cannibal King?" Shane asked.

"This is Death," Hugh replied.

The monstrous bellow echoed throughout the woods for a third time. It was louder now than ever before and seemed like it came from multiple directions.

"Those ghosts were trying to kill me," Shane said. "I'm not going to risk my life to maintain the balance on an island where allowing a certain number of people to be killed regularly is part of that balance."

"That balance worked for years before you arrived," Hugh said. "A few people dying is a better price than everyone dying. But that's what is going to happen now. You should just leave this place. Take everyone and leave."

"We would if we could," Shane said. "It's not that easy."

"Why?" the ghost asked.

"Why? Because we need boats. At least a radio to call for help. We need to convince all these people to go. And we need to do it before everyone gets slaughtered."

"It would have been a wise idea to investigate this before killing the others. You've thrown them off. They used to be predictable. They used to have set patterns. Now, with fewer of them, they don't know what to do with themselves. That's why the killing has increased. And that is why the other one is free now. You have created chaos for nothing."

The ghost seemed disinterested, despite the content of what he was saying. His voice was monotone. It seemed like he didn't care, even though his words dripped with condemnation.

"I can't predict what they're going to do anymore. They made my work easier before. They split up the forest. They had their territory. I watched them more easily and kept them apart from each other. I could keep them on task if it came to that. This isn't the first time the other one has tried to get out. He does it all the time. The difference was, I could wrangle them. Now, I don't know what to do."

"So, you've been herding these ghosts against the other spirit this whole time?" Frank asked.

"Only when needed. He sleeps, it seems. He waits. It can be years. He's very patient. He'll wait for a change. New people, a storm, something unusual to see if he can use it to cover his escape. And then, if they haven't stopped him, I will bring them to him. He can't manage against them all, so he backs down. It has been that way for a long time."

"How do you know he's so dangerous if he's never been loose?" Shane asked.

"I never said he hasn't been loose," Hugh replied. "I know why he needs to be held back *because* he's been loose."

"What happened?" Frank asked.

The ghost looked at him, his expression conveying a lot without saying words. He thought it was a stupid question.

"You mean aside from when he killed me? Long ago, back when ships ran on steam, people came to the island the way they always do. But they went north, they didn't go to the village. They never even looked. They set up camp on the north tip by the sea. The others were used to being here, in the south. The north was his land. So, he ventured up instead of down and they never knew. I saw him, though. I saw him tear every one of those men apart with his hands. I saw him use his bone blade and shave meat from bone."

"So, he did what they do," Shane said. He had expected that the ghost was a killer, so that was hardly a surprise. "He's a killer."

"You are not understanding," Hugh said, fixing his gaze on Shane. "He ripped them apart with his hands. He lifted them, full-grown men, into the air and he pulled their limbs from their bodies like they were twigs off branches. He pulled their spines from their backs, breaking ribs like they were made of fine porcelain. He is not like the others. He is a force of evil the likes of which I have never seen in life or death. If there is a devil, I think he would never tread on this land for fear of that thing which is now unleashed. That is what I am telling you."

The ghost let loose its roar again. The sound came from everywhere at once. Shane stiffened and balled his hands into fists. He was certain that the thing was upon them, that it was right outside of the juniper trees in which they hid. The force of the call made his teeth chatter and his flesh shift with goosebumps. He saw in Frank's eyes that his friend felt the same. Only Hugh seemed entirely calm, not worried about what was happening.

Shane looked through the branches, expecting to see this terrible spirit somewhere, but there was nothing. No movement, no indication that it was anywhere near as close as it sounded.

"Where is it?" Shane whispered.

"Don't know. It does not travel with its voice."

"What?"

"You will see it and not hear it. Hear it and not see it. It plays cruel games. I imagine it's on the way to the village if it can escape the others. With only four, it can probably kill them all. If you want to save anyone, we should start soon," Hugh said.

"Then what are we waiting for?" Shane asked.

"Had to make sure it wasn't going to tear your heads off first," the ghost explained. He stood up then and made his way out of the shrubs. "I will show you the way."

CHAPTER 16
CHOOSE OR DIE

Hugh led them south. They were at a remote, northwestern corner of the woods, somewhere that should have been extremely far from their actual position. Shane was still not sure how the ghosts had pulled off the illusion or how they had covered so much ground without realizing it, but he could do little about it now.

"If you are going to take everyone from here, I will help you," Hugh said. "It's the only way this can work now."

"That's been our plan since yesterday," Frank assured the ghost. "We didn't want more people to die."

"Your plan is not going well," the ghost said.

"We noticed," Shane replied.

They had returned to the portion of the woods where the trees were being tapped, and aluminum buckets hung from the sides. They were still close enough to the shore to hear the water as it crashed against the rocks below.

"None of this matters if we have no boats," Shane pointed out. "Do you know where they are?"

"In the water," Hugh said.

Shane resisted the urge to fire a smart comment back, instead glancing at Frank, who shrugged.

"They moved them from the docks. The sooner we find them, the sooner we can all get out of your hair."

"That is reasonable," Hugh said. They trudged onward through the trees, the ghost pausing every so often to listen to sounds that Shane could not hear.

"Does that mean you're going to help?" he asked.

"I do not want people to die the way I died. I would not wish this on my worst enemy. And yet it happens again and again despite my efforts. Take the people from this place. I will help you if you can do that."

"We will," Frank assured him.

Shane felt his jaw tense. He wouldn't have made the same assurance. Not with how many people were still resisting leaving the island. There was no guarantee that everyone would go. In fact, he was sure that not everyone wanted to.

"The easiest way to make sure this never happens again is to get rid of the ghosts, not the people," Shane said.

Hugh looked at him oddly, the same perplexing look the ghost had on his face when they fought.

"You do not listen," he said.

"I've heard you. I just don't think your problem-solving skills are the best. There are four ghosts left, five if you count Mr. Screams-a-lot. With your help, we can destroy them, and then it won't matter who comes to the island."

Hugh's teeth chattered, and it reminded Shane of the other spirits in an unsettling way.

"He is not something I can fight," Hugh said, referring to the Cannibal King. "He is not something anyone can fight."

"Let's not get ahead of ourselves," Shane said.

"We've been over this. You couldn't even defeat me. He will tear your head from your shoulders. Both of you."

Shane chuckled wryly, a twinge of aggravation growing.

"We never finished a fight, but the closest we got was me almost destroying you," he said.

"We didn't finish before because I didn't want you dead," the ghost said.

Frank gave Shane a sharp look. He didn't want this to continue. They didn't need to antagonize Hugh.

"The three of us together should be able to take out Mr. Hungry if he's that big of a menace."

Shane was acquiescing to Frank. He didn't think he would need help to take on this Cannibal King, despite what Hugh seemed to think. While the ghost was right—Shane had never defeated him—it didn't mean much. They had never finished their fight. And the ghost had no idea what Shane had done in the past. He had met more than his fair share of ghosts who were convinced of their supreme power and indestructibility. One more would not make a difference.

"The men in that building will be the first to die," Hugh said as they reached the forest's edge and the snow fields beyond. He was pointing east to the sugar shack, though they were too far from it to even see it now.

Shane wanted to say "good" but held his tongue. As much as he hated Lonnie, Hugh was right. Being eaten alive was not a good way to go. If nothing else, Shane could break his fingers this time and still be doing him a favor.

"We'll need to catch them by surprise. There are three guns between them… that we know of," Shane said.

"I have seen many armed men die on this island," Hugh said.

"Not *you* I'm worried about," Shane replied.

The three of them continued south, staying as far out of range of the sugar shack as they could, and then began the slow shift to the east, circling their destination. Shane doubted they had anyone else on guard duty. It was probably still Lonnie. But there was a chance they had now taken it more seriously since his capture and what they had seen. Better safe than sorry, Shane figured, and better to waste time staying out of sight.

Hugh kept a rigorous pace, aware of how slow the two living men had to go but also not caring very much. He glided through the snow, his legs from the shins down immersed in it, forcing them to travel at a slow run if they wanted to keep up.

He took them along the underside of a small hill, a little more than a slope in the landscape, but one that kept them well out of sight of the sugar shack while getting them closer than they might have been able to otherwise.

When they were close enough, Shane saw they had posted a second guard, this one at the back of the building. Six people were in there, and they still only had two on guard after everything that had just happened. Remarkable people, Shane thought.

Lonnie was still stationed out front, and an older man waited out back with a rifle slung over his shoulder.

"Third gunman must be back inside," Frank observed.

"Probably got cold feet," Shane said.

The harrowing sound returned from the woods. Shane watched as snow fell from the roof of the sugar shack, vibrating free under the force of the resonant bellow that erupted from the ghost somewhere far off in the woods. Or maybe not that far. Hugh said it did not appear where the sound appeared; it had some ghostly ability to throw its voice.

Shane saw Lonnie tense at the sound. The man held his gun like he might break it in half, but he had no idea where to aim it, not that it would have done him any good. Even if a ghost could be shot, Lonnie would still die if that was his only defense. He couldn't hit a target to save his life.

The man from the rear of the shack came around to join Lonnie. They must have been talking about what they heard and what it meant. They had to know what it was. Maybe not specifically, but they had to know it was a ghost. Why any of these people wanted to stay on the island was beyond Shane's understanding.

He knew many of them were misfits. They had issues in their past lives. They were lost. But now, they were being eaten. It was mind-blowing that people could make such terrible choices. People would willingly put their lives at risk because they thought they were in the right place and doing the right thing.

Normally, Shane wouldn't have cared that much, but some people on the island didn't know what they were getting into. Some had been lied to by Mallory about what was happening. Shane didn't care if the rest wanted to die, but if it was part of the deal to get Hugh's help, to clear the island, save everyone, and maybe get rid of the ghosts at the same time, then he would fight an idiot like Lonnie just to save his life.

They watched, and the new guard and Lonnie stayed out front together. The sound of the ghost faded, and silence covered the world like that blanket of snow again.

"Flank?" Shane suggested to Frank, then adding for Hugh. "You take the guns."

"Very well," Hugh said, "but this will need to be swift. I do not think we have much time."

"It'll go faster if they can't shoot us," Shane assured him.

They made their way to the rear of the sugar shack, staying out of sight until they could use the building for cover. Frank headed to the north end while Shane took the south. They waited as Hugh made his way to where the two men waited. The ghost remained unseen by the guards.

Hugh could only be seen by the others when he wanted to be, so the ghost could walk up to both men unseen and pull the guns from their hands before they realized what was happening.

From the perspective of Lonnie and his partner, the guns in their hands were simply pulled away by the wind, hurled backward into the snow, and lost in a sea of white. The men had little time to react or be surprised by what had happened before Shane and Frank were on them.

The unknown guard was confused at first, but he seemed ready for a fight. Lonnie, on the other hand, ran. The snow had been well-trampled, however, and Shane caught up with him quickly. He tackled Lonnie before the door to the sugar shack and gagged him with his scarf again. Frank took down the second man soon after, but he couldn't silence him. The guard screamed for help as Shane bound Lonnie's ankles and pulled the loose end forward.

The door to the shack opened, and a third man stood there, dumbstruck, staring at Shane as he tied Lonnie's hands with his scarf.

"Dave! Dave, it's them!" the man at the door shouted.

A fourth man appeared, presumably Dave, and he had the last rifle in his hands as he stepped outside to confront Shane and Frank. He must have not understood the first man's warning and thought their targets were far away. He was surprised to see Shane in front of him and brought the rifle to bear.

Shane left Lonnie hogtied on the ground and stood swiftly, driving the butt of the rifle into Dave's face and causing him to collapse next to his friend.

Once he took control, Shane turned the rifle around, aimed it at the man in the shack, and then took a step back.

"Call your friends out or your head gets a new hole," Shane told him.

"Guys!" the man said obediently. "You gotta come quickly!"

Two more men came to the door and immediately put their hands up. Shane stepped back to allow them room and used the gun to gesture past Lonnie and Dave. They got out of the sugar shack, hands raised, with panicked expressions. This was not the A-Team.

"Please, man, this wasn't even my idea," the fifth man said.

"Shut up," Shane told him.

Frank brought the other man over, but they left Lonnie on the ground next to Dave, who had at least sat up and was tending to his bloody nose. The other men stood around him, and no one offered to help Lonnie or Dave, not that Shane would have let them. Lonnie needed some time to think. Dave was just unlucky.

"I'm going to give you boys a choice," Shane said.

He still held the gun, though he was not pointing it at anyone. He held it ready, off to the side, responsible enough not to aim it at a man he didn't plan to shoot.

"I didn't come here to kill anybody. I admit, you people have been pissing me off, and I'd just as soon leave you all here to rot, but this isn't just my call. You are all going to die if you stay here. But if you come with us, we can take your boats, get everyone off this island, and no one else has to die."

"Why the hell would we go anywhere with you?" one of the men asked Shane.

"Because the guys who killed him will come for you if you don't," he answered, gesturing to his left.

Hugh approached the group and to Shane's eyes, nothing changed. But the men could see him now.

Lonnie was the first to scream.

CHAPTER 17

TRUCE

"Oh Jesus, God, please don't kill me! Please don't kill me!"

Lonnie blubbered into the snow, spit and snot and tears running down his face as though the world were ending, and he was the last man to witness the destruction of everything. Shane sighed and let him go for a few moments. He tried to remember what it must have been like to see a ghost like Hugh for the first time. It certainly would have been terrifying, and Hugh was an especially unpleasant-looking spirit. He was a walking nightmare, or would have been to most people. Most normal people.

"Lonnie, settle down," Shane said.

The man was still whimpering as Shane knelt in the snow next to him.

"If he wanted you dead, he would have chewed your face right off while you struggled here like a trussed-up little ham, don't you think?"

Shane looked up at the others.

"This is what they do to you. This is what happened to every single one of the people Mallory sacrificed to this island. This guy isn't doing it; it was done to him. Long before any of us existed. Do any of you want to feel what that felt like?"

He pointed at Hugh, and the villagers said nothing. Half couldn't even look at him, terror had gripped them so badly. Only one man, the last to exit the shack and the oldest by far, shook his head in the negative.

"We need the boats to leave this place. I need someone to tell me where they are or you're all going to be eaten. Literally eaten. Are we all on the same page?"

Shane spoke to them like they were children, hoping the message would sink in. The visual Hugh provided was invaluable. Shane could talk until he was blue in the face about dying and Mallory sacrificing people haphazardly, but looking at an animated, cannibalized corpse was a pretty good way to get a message across in very few words.

"Blaine took them," the old man who shook his head said. "Blaine and Grady and Stacks. They left with the boats, so you need to ask them."

"Stacks and Grady are dead," Lonnie said weakly. "They got killed last night."

"Blaine, then," the old man said. "He's your man. Or Mallory. She knows everything."

Shane sighed loudly and looked at Frank.

"You getting all this?"

"Someone else has to know," Frank said. "Does Blaine have any friends?"

"Stacks," the old man said. "And Grady."

"Jesus," Shane whispered.

"Blaine is dead," Frank informed the group. "So is Mallory."

"Oh, God…" the old man said.

The others were still too afraid to speak. Shane wanted to throw all of them into the sea, use their corpses as a raft, and just paddle to shore. He was done with the island and its small, bothersome populace.

"If Blaine took the boats and was still here, then the boats have to still be here, right?" Shane said. "They have to be docked somewhere else."

"Never saw no other dock here," the old man said.

"Lonnie? You ever see another dock?"

"No," he whimpered. "I swear I never did."

"And you never looked?" Shane was talking to Hugh this time.

The ghost glowered.

"No."

"*Can* you? You help us, we help you, remember?"

"I can only travel so far. I am bound to the village. The northern shore is beyond my reach, but I will look where I can."

"And you guys?" Shane turned back to the villagers. "You going to help? Or do you want to shoot at me again, and let his ghost friends have their way with you?"

He jerked a thumb toward Hugh. The ghost did not like being lumped in with the others, but he let the comment slide.

"I'll help you," the old man said. "I came here for peace. For a place to live the way folks used to. But it ain't that anymore."

Shane looked at the other men.

"Just take me back to the mainland," the next man said, and his companion nodded.

"I'll help you," another man added.

Shane looked at Dave and Lonnie.

"I'll do anything, just please, don't kill me," Lonnie begged.

Dave frowned through the crusted blood across his nose and mouth, and nodded.

"I'm in, I guess."

"Look at us. We've got ourselves a team," Shane said.

The Cannibal King bellowed again from deep in the forest, the sound traveling through the ground and causing the muscles in Shane's legs to vibrate. He saw that everyone else felt it, too, and the panic on Lonnie's face increased. Before the cry died out, it was answered by a high-pitched shriek. The sound was different, not from the same voice, and it came from elsewhere in the woods.

Shane looked at Hugh, and the ghost had turned to face the forest, half in a crouch the way he liked to sit, with his bony knees up.

"That was one of them," Hugh said. "They've found him."

"What will happen?" Frank asked.

"They'll fight if they can. With so few, I don't know what will happen. They might flee, or he might destroy them all right now. If he does, we will have precious little time to escape. We must move and move now."

"You go north," Frank said. "I'll take these men back to the village. We can take Mallory's body and the two dead elders. They won't look at me as harshly as they will look at you."

Shane couldn't argue the point. He was, in most people's eyes, Mallory's murderer. Frank was the guy who everyone had gotten to know while making dinner. And now that they had a few of the locals on their side, it might grease the wheels.

"We'll head north, then," Shane said, half a question for Hugh's benefit. The ghost didn't acknowledge him, but Shane took it as acceptance since he didn't shoot the idea down. "If the boats are docked somewhere, we'll find them."

"Meet here?"

"The village," Shane said. "I'll find you. Find a radio if you can, ransack Mallory's place if you have to. Mo might have come back this way, and he should have his ears on since he didn't see us. Someone is getting everyone off this island."

"Don't get killed," Frank advised.

"Going to do my best." Shane put his hand out to Dave, who was still sitting in the snow. The other man was hesitant but took it, and Shane helped the man to his feet.

"We need to work together, or a lot of people die." Shane held out the rifle, and Dave stared at it suspiciously before slowly taking it. "Might as well untie Lonnie, too. He doesn't look like he can run fast right now."

One of the men untied the scarf and helped Lonnie back to his feet.

"Can I have my gun back?" Lonnie asked after straightening his scarf.

"If you can find it," Shane told him. "Won't do you much good, though. That sound you've been hearing is what killed all these other guys. This one here is worse than the ones that take the people from the village. Bullets won't stop him."

"Let's get the bodies of your friends and bring them home," Frank said, rounding up the villagers. They fell in line quickly, none eager to stay with Hugh.

Frank left with a final nod to Shane, and the group trudged through the field toward where the three bodies had been left. Shane left them to it, heading north while Hugh joined him.

"You seem like you don't want to help these people, and yet you are. Why do you do it if you don't care what happens to them?" the ghost asked.

He kept pace with Shane at his side but did not look at him. He was slower than he had been, and Shane wondered if part of him was trying to waste time. If part of him did not want to confront the ghost in the forest.

"Same reason you're doing it," Shane told him. "I wanna get this over with. I'm sick of dealing with the hassle. If I can get everyone off this island, and maybe get rid of the rest of these ghosts so no one else has an issue in the future, then I can go home and enjoy my coffee."

"That is not my reason for doing any of this," Hugh replied.

"Close enough," Shane said.

He stopped then and unzipped his coat, reached inside his chest pocket, and pulled out his pack of cigarettes. He hadn't had a chance to smoke in far too long, and he was avoiding doing it out in the wild because he didn't want the villagers to see where he was. Now that it was no longer a concern, he planned on at least enjoying himself a little.

"Is that tobacco?" Hugh asked as Shane placed the cigarette between his lips.

"The finest grown in Argentina, Mozambique, Brazil, the USA, and maybe a half-dozen other countries."

"My father grew tobacco," Hugh said. "I haven't smoked in so long."

He had a longing in his voice as Shane lit the cigarette and inhaled deeply, then exhaled.

"I'd offer you a puff, but I don't think it'd do much for you."

"No," Hugh agreed. "I imagine not."

They continued walking again, with Hugh leading them slightly to the northeast as they went. He seemed to be circumnavigating the forest as best he could. The trees were much patchier to the east, giving way almost entirely along the eastern wall, though they did not stray that far.

"How far north can you go?"

"Until I can't any longer," the ghost replied.

"Ask a stupid question," Shane muttered. "How much ground am I going to have to cover on my own?"

"I can't say. I've never covered it."

"Right."

Hugh was not the best at small talk or strategy. At least he was good in a fight. Shane hoped he was as good against the others. If he couldn't hold his own against the dead, he was losing a lot of appeal as a partner.

"We will need to be cautious when we get to the north. It is their territory as much as it is his. They are rooted in the woods. I am rooted in the village. They could always travel farther north than I could. I don't know what they do out there."

"I found a tree filled with skulls once, after you tossed me off that ridge. Stuff like that what you're talking about? Or something else?"

"Worse things," the ghost answered.

They walked in silence for a while longer until Shane had finished his cigarette. They were much closer to the eastern wall now, and Shane recognized the pathway to the cave that he had taken with Frank. They passed by it and continued, heading into land that Shane had never explored.

"If you've never been up that far, how do you know it's worse?" Shane asked.

"Sound," Hugh answered. "On a still night, sound travels very well on the island. I heard them sometimes on the days new people arrived. New ships that came to explore, their crews eager to see what the island had to offer. Some nights, I heard what was happening."

"And it was worse than what I've already seen?"

"If they got them in the north, they knew I could not intervene, so they didn't need to rush. They might seem like animals, but they are men. When they had the time and patience, they could keep a man alive for days."

Shane nodded. That, he understood. Their savagery was a product of circumstance. They killed quickly because they feared Hugh would stop them. Without that fear, they were patient.

"So, I should not get caught in the north," Shane said.

"You should use your weapon and kill yourself first if you get caught in the north," Hugh answered.

CHAPTER 18

THE NORTH

For the first time, the forest showed diverse growth. Tall cedars, aspens, and ash seemed to have carved their space away from the maple forest.

The trees were not densely packed along the path to the northeast. Much of the land was flat and snow-covered, with several yards between the random trees. As a result of the spacing, many had grown very tall. Their trunks were covered in light, silvery bark that peeled off in curls and reminded Shane of flaking skin.

Even though the maple forest was free of leaves, the trees still looked alive and healthy. Here, the trees had a more wretched quality. Maybe it was the peeling bark or the proximity to the shore where the wind had affected how they grew, but most of the trees were bent, their branches curled inward like bony, arthritic hands forming fists.

Soon enough, it became clear that the trees were no longer alive; just dead, skeletal forms that dotted the landscape. Birch trees had twisted and nearly doubled over on themselves, their papery bark hanging off them in long, winding strips. They reminded Shane of Hugh and the other ghosts. Like they had been surgically cut apart, skinned alive, and left as nightmare versions of what they had been in life.

"We are in his lands," Hugh said by way of explanation. "I try not to come this far north. The others used to be able to keep him here."

They walked another twenty yards in silence. Shane did not know if Hugh saw what was ahead of them first, but neither he nor the ghost said anything as they approached a large cedar tree that had been stripped of all its lower branches.

Something was in the tree, just more than ten feet off the ground. There was no snow on it, even though the branches farther up and on nearby trees had a light dusting. The shape on the tree was clean as though someone had maintained it, dusting it off to make sure it was seen. There were no tracks in the snow around the base course.

Shane and Hugh slowed their approach. The shape attached to the tree was a human body. The flesh on the corpse was not unlike the bark of the tree. It looked dry and flaky like it had been out in the sun for a very long time. It was old and seemed to be almost mummified, but its exact age was a mystery.

There were no legs on the figure; they looked to have been torn away a long time ago. What remained had been partially dissected. Half of the chest was missing, not just the skin and muscle, but the bone as well. The left side of the rib cage had been cut and removed, exposing the interior of the dead man's chest.

There was no way to know if the organs had rotted away or had been removed, but the interior of the chest cavity was empty. Half of the ribs at the back, attached to the spine, were still present. The cuts that had taken the rest of the bones were not clean and smooth. It looked like they might have even been broken, jagged and splintered at some points.

The dead man on the tree still had a face. It had not been badly wounded from what Shane saw. However, years of being outside in the sun and in the salt air off the sea had preserved it in a ghastly fashion. Darkened, stained flesh like jerky clung tightly around the empty eye sockets and missing nose. The mouth of the corpse hung open, giving it an expression like it was caught in an endless scream. Across the cheeks, it was bunched up tightly along the edges, but thin and yellowed everywhere else.

The body had been impaled on a pair of broken branches, stabbed through the back of the ribs in two places that likely would have hit the heart and lungs if they had been present when the man was attached. Shane did not think that was how the man died. He guessed that the man was tortured extensively first, and then probably hung up after he had died.

The hanging corpse was not alone. Hugh kept walking, and Shane followed at his side, discovering more trees like the first one. The next body they saw was nearly whole. The dead man had his legs this time, but his chest had been removed. Shane couldn't say where the rib cage was, but he guessed that the man's insides had been pulled out by whoever had done it to him. He was impaled through his face on a branch rather than his chest.

On a smaller ash tree, closer to the rocky ledge that looked out over the eastern sea, Shane saw a body that had been peeled off of all its flesh. The muscle had been left behind, and it had dried dark and ropey, but the skin itself had been removed, taken down the length of the body, and left to hang from the dead man's ankles. It still hung there, shredded and dried up like old parchment paper.

Had the island any wildlife, any insects or predators, the bodies would have been savaged long ago. The insects and animals could not resist fresh meat. But, just as with Shane's home in Nashua, the island was devoid of life. The presence of ghosts kept life from taking root. Nothing wanted to live so close to death. And so, nature had preserved the bodies and left them there to be seen by anyone brave or foolish enough to walk so far north.

"Who are these people?" Shane asked.

They were not the ghosts he had seen. They were not Hugh Carson or the other spirits that he had tangled with. These men had been killed very differently, and their bodies were left in vastly different conditions.

None Shane saw had clothing. There was no way to date them based on external factors. The preservation meant they could have been ten, or two hundred years old; there was no way to know.

"Dead men," Hugh answered unhelpfully.

"Clearly," Shane replied.

"The island is not remote. It's not hard to get here. I have seen ships steer wide around the island for no reason. There's something about it that keeps most people away. There's something here that makes people not want to be here. I think they feel an instinct, something deep in their soul, when they see this place. But for some, it does not work. Some see this island and view it as an opportunity. So, they bring their boats to shore and often lose them on the rocks. It is the island's way of punishing those who don't listen to the voice in their soul telling them to stay away. Once they are here, they don't leave."

"So even you think the island has willpower," Shane said.

"I have to," Hugh said. "If there is no will here, then I am a fool who stumbled into this horror for nothing. Nothing I do matters. My life didn't matter. No life does."

Shane chuckled, and Hugh glared at him.

"That amuses you?"

"You're very dour. I know some ghosts who would love to spend time with you."

"I have had my fill of the dead," Hugh replied, taking him seriously.

"I bet," Shane said.

They passed more of the dead men nailed to trees. No two were alike. Some were heads with spines attached, and some were just skeletons. Once, three legs were impaled on the same branch and nothing else. Shane counted at least three dozen bodies.

He wondered how long people had been coming to the island. Hugh must have been there for over two hundred years if he had been part of the fur trade, and the Cannibal King that he feared had already been there at that time. The ghosts on the island were going back before the United States was even a country. Three hundred? Four hundred years?

"You said this Cannibal King has a blade?" Shane asked.

"Made of bone, yes," Hugh said. "Sharp as steel."

Maybe it was nothing, but tools made of bone could have been thousands of years old. It was rare to find a ghost that old, but it was not unheard of. The Cannibal King could have been on the island long before Europeans found the continent.

The age of the ghost didn't matter, Shane supposed, but he had learned that the older a spirit was, the craftier it tended to be. Often, it was much stronger, too. Just like a living man, years gave a ghost wisdom.

This ghost could have just as easily been only a few years older than Hugh. He could have just been a fan of primitive weapons, a sadist who found something that amused him. Either explanation was plausible. Shane didn't plan to talk to him to find out one way or the other.

"How many men have you seen come to the island since you've been here?" Shane asked.

"Three hundred, perhaps. Fully crewed ships for most of those years. But later ones, like the people who are here now, came one at a time. The King made a mistake by killing so many. He made his own jailers, and the death stopped. But the world had changed by then. Fewer people came here. Fewer ships dashed on the rocks. The numbers dwindled. Now, it is only one new soul every few months, if that. And they live in their village, throw a new body to the wild ones when the season is right, and everything stays the same."

It sounded like a lot. Three hundred people murdered by ghosts on an island where no one would ever come to find them. They were likely considered lost at sea. If anyone came looking, they would have found the wrecked ships and assumed the ocean had taken them. Maybe if they reached the land, they would have looked around, seen nothing, and left empty-handed.

The cannibals and this Cannibal King had found a unique pocket in the world. A place where laws didn't apply, where no one would investigate anything suspicious, and where death could continue not just easily but happily. Willingly. Shane had never encountered anything like it.

"The only way to end this is to destroy them all," Shane said. "If we don't, people will keep coming. For as many people as this island keeps away, there will be those who can't resist it. You're right; there is something. There's an allure, a pull that the dead have on some people. I've seen it myself. It's like they can't resist."

"Who are you that you know so much of the dead? That you can fight them?" Hugh's lack of curiosity only extended so far.

"Just someone who sees things for what they are."

"Is this what you do? You hunt the dead?"

"Sometimes," Shane said.

"Are you good at it?"

Shane laughed.

"Not dead yet."

Hugh nodded as he stopped next to a tree adorned with the headless body of what was once a very short man.

"There is no point in me following you further. I have nearly reached my limit. You will have to inspect the north on your own from here. I will look along the eastern shores for your boats. If you live, I will find you when you return," the ghost said.

"Goodbye to you too, Hugh," Shane said, but the ghost was already gone, vanished over the eastern ridge.

Shane looked north. More bodies on trees awaited, and the sound of his feet crunching snow.

CHAPTER 19

LIES AND HARD TRUTHS

Frank stood with his hands up as the man who had chased them from the village with Clint pointed the barrel of a rifle in his face.

"Where's Ryan?" The man demanded.

"North," Frank answered. "We can talk if you want to lower that."

"I don't," the man said.

"You gotta listen to him," said the old man from the sugar shack, who Frank now knew as Jones. "You don't know what we saw out there."

"I know what I saw here," the armed man said. "His friend killed Mallory. Shot her in cold blood."

"He didn't!" Clint shouted. "You ask anyone who was in there. It wasn't him who did it. It was Gareth with Shane's gun. He picked it up off the floor, shot at Shane, missed, and killed Mallory. Everyone saw it."

There were few people on the street in the town when Frank returned. He imagined the attack from the ghost had scared most of them indoors. Seeing the ghosts carry away one of their own, kicking and screaming, must have been more than most people could bear. But Clint had still been outside. He greeted Frank when he returned with the others. Unfortunately, the homecoming was short-lived.

Before he had gone even ten yards into the village, Frank was stopped with a gun in his face. Blaine's old supporters, and Mallory's, had come out to confront him. But Frank was happy to see those from the sugar shack standing by him. He had been afraid that they would turn on him once they returned to town. Seeing the ghost of Hugh Carson had clearly affected the men.

"He's telling the truth," someone shouted, leaving their cabin. Frank recognized her as Judith. He had spoken to her on the first day. She had been in Mallory's cabin.

Others echoed the sentiment, and the man with the gun began to look unsure. Still, his anger controlled his actions more than rationality or listening to the people around him.

"It was his gun," the man said. "Mallory would still be alive if not for him. He's got to account for that."

"Who accounts for Blaine?" Jones asked.

The armed man's brow furrowed, and he looked at his fellow villager.

"The hell are you talking about, Jones?"

"He's dead, isn't he? Who killed him?"

"I got no idea where Blaine is. Haven't seen him all day," the man replied.

"He's dead," Clint said. "I saw them come for him in the night. They dragged him out of town. Just like they took Miriam today. And Mallory."

More of the villagers had come to the streets to see what was happening. Some of them gasped at the news from Clint, shocked and saddened. Others whispered things to each other. The tides were turning, but they had not succeeded in getting everyone to see the truth just yet.

"It doesn't matter what happened before," Lonnie piped up in front of the others. "We saw what's out there, and it ain't Frank or his asshole friend. They weren't lying. That thing? It's not the island spirit. It's not here to help us. If anything, it's the devil in those woods, and Mallory's been feeding us to it this whole time."

Alina appeared on the streets, and Frank was relieved to see she was still okay. He still had his hands up, was still standing at gunpoint, and still hoping that cooler heads were going to prevail.

The man wielding the gun had others with him, men and women Frank recognized from the cabin when Mallory died. People who knew the truth but chose to believe that Frank and Shane were responsible. People who, even hearing their fellow villagers tell them what was going on, didn't want to accept the truth.

Frank considered it a victory that anyone had changed their mind. The right move seemed obvious, but these people had committed a life to their island. And not just that, but they had committed their belief that dying was necessary to keep the place thriving. Had that not been part of it, had Mallory kept it a secret, anything different might have made his job easier.

The villagers had become a cult in a way. They were fanatics willing to sacrifice themselves for what they thought was a greater good. Or at least in theory. Frank doubted many would volunteer to be taken by the ghosts, but they were willing to have others volunteer. He didn't blame anyone for that. It was much easier to allow someone to sacrifice themselves for you than the other way around. It might have been cowardly, but it was human nature, and it was to be expected.

"We need to let the police sort it out," someone yelled. The crowd grew larger, and more voices joined in.

"Send them home on the boats," somebody else said.

"We *all* need to leave," Alina yelled. "This island isn't safe anymore."

It never was, Frank thought, but he did not want to be an agitator.

"Safe? Jesus, you people aren't listening." Jones spoke loudly to everyone. "That thing they showed us was like nothing I ever saw. I never knew those people who went missing... I never knew that was what happened to them. I thought Mallory banished them or they just ran off. I never thought it was real. I would have never stayed here if I knew..."

"The hell are you even talking about, Jones? Jesus, we're talking about these guys! About Mallory and Blaine and—"

"It's a goddamn ghost, Mitch! A dead... thing. A monster!"

"Jones—"

"I saw it with my eyes out there. We all saw it."

"We saw it here, too. Two nights ago." Alina said. "You know you did. Most of us did. It was here in the village. It fought with Shane."

Frank kept his hands up and said nothing. He had been going over in his head what he might say to convince people, what he could possibly do to get everyone on his side and willing to leave, but this was better. It was better if they talked among themselves, with people they already knew and trusted. Anything he said would be met with abject suspicion. He was an outsider, and he was friends with a man they were still insisting killed Mallory, even though they knew it was a lie.

If Jones, Alina, Lonnie, and the others convinced enough people—ones who had already seen Hugh in town or the others dragging their friends away that morning—they would be easier to sway. And the more people who were on their side, the easier it would be to convince those who weren't. Even if they didn't want to believe the truth, it was not hard to go with the majority. Frank didn't care why the people left, he just needed them to tell him where the boats were and then help get everyone out.

"Answer me this." The man with the gun pointed it back into Frank's face. "If this ghost is what's killing everyone, why was it with them? How come it didn't kill none of you?"

He looked at Frank but directed the question to Jones and Lonnie and the others. It was a valid concern, but Frank was surprised the man had thought to even ask.

"What if we all go to the Great Hall, get warm by the fire, and I will answer any questions I can?" Frank suggested.

"You can answer me here," Mitch said. Frank wanted to call the man by his name; it usually helped put people at ease, but he thought better of it. Mitch was angry and suspicious. Frank didn't want to come off patronizing.

"God, Mitch, we're all freezing. I've been in the snow for hours, man. Let's go in," Lonnie said.

The other men were on board and, while Frank still had his hands up, Jones put an arm around his shoulder and led him toward the Great Hall at the end of the road they were on.

Frank moved with him, reluctantly taking his eyes off Mitch and his gun. He was not inclined to turn his back on a man who had a weapon on him under normal circumstances, but he felt like the others around him would offer a reasonable amount of protection against him being shot. He didn't want to use the villagers as human shields, he was just hoping Mitch had the wherewithal to not start firing.

As it happened, Frank was right. Mitch, though angry, put up his gun and followed behind the others. The hall was the only building in the village large enough to hold everyone.

Frank smelled a meal being cooked when he entered. One of the cooks looked out of the kitchen, surprised by the crowd flowing into the building, but said nothing before he ducked back into the rear.

Thanks to several fires burning, the building was very warm and comfortable once they were all inside. Frank stayed at the head of the first table, standing rather than sitting, and looking as non-threatening as he could.

Jones and the other men sat near him, and Mitch sat with them but laid the gun across the table rather than hold it. The barrel was pointed away from Frank, and he took that as a good sign. Still, Mitch and those who were with him looked at Frank with naked suspicion. They were not ready to believe anything he said yet. Maybe not ever.

"Your island is haunted," Frank said.

The people of the town had been talking among themselves, and the murmur of conversation died out almost immediately in the Great Hall. Clint and Alina sat near Frank with the others who supported him, but everyone had something to say. Frank's words shut them all up.

"Mallory was not lying when she spoke to you of a spirit, but she also did not know the whole truth. These cabins were built by men long ago. First the stone ones and then the wood. Some of them were traders; others were trappers, working between Maine and Nova Scotia before either had a name. Something here killed them. More than one thing is here now."

"The hell does that even mean?" Mitch asked.

"Death begets death. Something was here. A man from long ago. We think he was stranded on this island after his boat was smashed on the rocks. Winter came, and he and his companions resorted to the unthinkable. They began to eat their dead. At some point, this spirit that is here killed those who were still alive and ate them. But he eventually ran out of anything to eat, and he died. His spirit returned to haunt this place."

The assorted villagers murmured and whispered. Frank saw that Mitch did not believe a word of it. Others looked horrified.

"More men came, and this ghost killed them. And he relived what he had done in the past. He butchered them and ate them even though their meat could not nourish him anymore. Eventually, there were more like him. Feral, mad spirits who had died in fear and agony. These are the things that Mallory has been feeding, thinking they were sustaining your way of life. But all she was doing was making them ignore you until the urge struck again. They were never responsible for the crops. They don't have that power. They are ghosts of dead men, not earth spirits like Mallory thought."

The whispering continued, and the shock and horror grew on people's faces.

"The ghost that some of you have seen, the one that helped me and Shane today, was another victim. A man named Hugh Carson, shipwrecked here long ago. He's been protecting you even if you never saw it. He tries to keep the others at bay. But the first ghost is free now, and no one can keep him in check any longer, and he will kill us all if we do not leave this island. And it will be a death worse than you can imagine."

Frank did not like scaring people or using words to intimidate them, but he needed these people to be scared. He needed them to understand the truth.

Most of all, he needed them to tell him where the boats were.

CHAPTER 20

IN THE VALLEY OF THE SHADOW

Shane stopped suddenly. He had been fishing around in his pocket for another cigarette. But something had changed.

He had been approaching some poplar trees and a twisted, dried-up body that was pinned to a branch a moment earlier. Only it was not there when he looked back up.

Shane removed his hand from his pocket and turned, looking at some of the trees behind him. Other bodies were also missing. The dead had vanished. They had not fallen to the ground. There were no tracks or signs of them, they were just gone.

"So, this is the game," he said softly.

They had not looked like ghosts to him when he'd seen them. They looked like bodies. Now, he suspected he was seeing both at the same time. The ghosts could have been inside their corpses, waiting for someone to come by. It must have been some time since anyone had traveled this far north. He was well past where the villagers tapped the maple trees to make syrup. And even if any of them had seen the bodies in the trees, they certainly would not have come back this way.

All it would take was one or two people traveling up the eastern coast of the island and never returning to convince the rest to never go this way. It might have been a standing rule back at the village for all he knew.

Nothing moved save for falling snow. Shane took off his gloves and flexed his fingers in the cold. He wondered how much time he had. He knew they were coming. Gathering. But how many? Dozens had been posted to the trees. He didn't think all of them were ghosts, but he wasn't certain.

The numbers did not favor Shane, even if only a fraction of the bodies were ghosts. He needed an advantage. The iron rings would not help if the trees and the bodies were the haunted items. He'd be sending them mere feet away.

He could run, but that would just waste time and energy. He might end up in a worse position with more of them, anyway. Only one option made sense to him.

Shane walked back toward the tree where the last dead body had been pinned a few moments earlier. He touched the trunk, stared up at the branches, and then looked around. Only his tracks in the snow marred the ground. But the snow was deep enough to hide almost anything. Certainly a ghost, or several.

"I don't have all day," he said. "Makes it easier if you just do it now."

Only the sound of the waves crashing against the distant, rocky shore of the island answered him. He took another step, away from the tree and back down the path he'd come from. Something clicked. It was a quick, repetitive tapping sound. Three or four in succession.

Shane's hands curled into fists, and he turned. The ghost behind him crawled from the snow, using its arms to dig itself out. It had legs but no feet. The skin on its back had been peeled away, revealing its spine and ribs. It scuttled toward Shane with remarkable speed for something that looked so dried up and desiccated.

The ghost's face was frozen in an expression that looked almost like mock ecstasy. The empty eye sockets looked like they were squinting with the way the flesh had sagged, and the crooked mouth hung open and drooped to one side.

Shane saw how this visage would terrify most, but he saw only the easy opportunity it presented.

The ghost came at him, and Shane moved to meet it. He sidestepped it easily, planting his foot on the ghost's back as he reached down and plunged two fingers into the empty eye sockets. He pulled as though lifting a bowling ball, and the ghost's dry body resisted as it struggled, which only helped Shane by loosening the brittle tendons and muscles. He dropped to his knee on the spirit's back, digging into its spine as he pulled up harder and wrenched its head from its body.

It took far less effort than Shane had expected to remove the ghost's head. Once he had it free, it fell apart with a simple squeeze, bursting with a weaker-than-typical rush of energy. It was as though the ghost had been used up, and there was very little left that kept it going.

There was no time to consider the implications of the fragile ghost. The sound of the crashing waves was overwhelmed with a chorus of clicks, moans, dry scratching sounds, and hissing. A cacophony of noise rose from the ground as the other corpses came for him, clawing, stumbling, and walking from their hiding places. Those that were able to be upright shambled toward him while the others crawled or dragged themselves.

A half-dozen came for Shane together. None moved with speed, and none even seemed to have an outward understanding of what they were doing. It was all mindless action borne of feral instinct. They reminded Shane of zombies in the movies. Shuffling, slow, empty, and driven by a sinister hunger that didn't make sense.

The first of the spirits reached him, and this one had nearly all its body intact. It wobbled like it might fall in either direction at any moment, and reached out with wiry, dried-up arms.

Shane grabbed the spirit by the wrist and pulled it toward him, wrapping one arm around its neck as it fell into him. He moved his body as the ghost dropped and took it down to the ground as he crushed its head. By the time he hit the snow, the ghost was gone.

The spirit's demise was as weak as the one before it. It was less explosive and more pathetic than any normal destruction should have been. The ghost came apart like someone bursting a balloon.

Shane wondered what could have happened to someone to leave them in such a state. If the Cannibal King was their killer, he wondered what the spirit had done to them while they were still alive. The torture must have been long and arduous. The brutal injuries they suffered had to have happened when they were still alive, and he must have kept them alive for some time.

Perhaps the torture was too much even for their ghosts. When they came back, they were only a shadow of what they should have been. The state of them all made it easy to imagine. Skin peeled off down to muscle. Whole rib cages pulled open and organs missing. If the ghost had kept them alive for even a fraction of it, they would have been as broken as the monsters that lived in the maple forest.

Shane had never encountered anything like it, but that didn't mean it wasn't possible. That someone could break down the will and the spirit of a person so badly as they tortured them until the moment of death that even their ghosts carried the trauma was remarkable. Maybe Hugh and the other spirits handled what happened better than the others. None of them seemed sane, but they still had willpower and drive. Maybe the ones pinned to the trees were the ones that gave up.

More of the dead appeared, clawing out of the ground or oozing out of trees. The numbers were intimidating, but they had proven to be weak and ineffectual. Shane brought the fight to them, not waiting to get overwhelmed. Even weak enemies could become a problem if their numbers built too much.

Shane stomped on the head of the nearest ghost, one of the more wretched creatures that was just half a torso with arms attached and an eyeless face. He crushed its head beneath his boot like it was nothing, and the blowback was barely enough to make him stumble.

The ghosts moaned, some producing sounds like dry heaves or retching. His concern was no longer the ghosts but why they had attacked him. It could have been his bad luck, just a coincidence walking through the woods. But it could have been something else. They were serving as a reasonable distraction.

If the Cannibal King was clever, he could use them as a trap. They certainly would have killed anyone walking through who didn't have Shane's abilities. But even for him, they represented a major distraction. And they would give anyone observing a chance to study him. If the Cannibal King was clever, that was.

As the density of ghosts increased, Shane found himself fighting two or three at a time. There were perhaps two dozen coming at him. The more that came, the slower he was in dealing with them, playing defense and offense simultaneously. He struck where he could, leveling crushing blows that broke bones or caved in skulls with single hits.

He saw that only portions of these dead had been eaten. Someone had shown restraint with them. They were not nearly as mangled as Hugh Carson and the others. The eating seemed secondary in these cases. The real goal seemed to have been torture. To inflict pain in as many cruel and brutal ways as possible.

Dry, gnarled bodies fell apart in Shane's hands. He tore them apart, using pieces of one to batter another. The final push came at him, with close to ten surrounding him, the last of what the forest had to offer.

Shane had kept his head on a swivel during the entire fight, looking for any sign of the King or the other monsters from the woods, but it seemed like nothing was there. No one was watching, and no one had set a trap for him. And then, as Shane wrenched the head from one of the final ghosts, he saw that he was not alone.

Hugh was watching from near the eastern ledge where rocks gave way to the sea. The ghost was just crouching there, the way he did all the time, with his legs bent like a demented frog. He watched Shane silently, not moving, unfazed, until the last of the decrepit ghosts had been destroyed.

Shane was breathing heavily, and misty clouds of white rose above his face as he took a moment after destroying the final spirit. He waited to see if more would come, if some had been slow to join the fray or had held back just in case. Nothing appeared. He had destroyed them all and could rest a moment, breathing the frigid air into his lungs as he watched Hugh watching him.

"Enjoying the show?" Shane shouted through the sparse trees to the ghost.

Hugh got to his feet and walked the short distance from where he had been watching to where Shane was now pulling a cigarette from his pocket. He watched the ghost carefully as he lit the tip and took a long drag.

"You did well enough," Hugh said.

Shane chuckled, taking the cigarette from between his lips.

"Glad you approved. This some kind of test for you?"

"No," Hugh answered. "I thought the others might come. These ones are slow and weak. I think they were somehow drained of their spirit. But the other ones are attracted to them. They come here sometimes."

"And you thought I'd make good bait," Shane said.

Hugh shrugged awkwardly with his mangled shoulders.

"Yes," he said.

"Could have told me."

"Most people do not want to be bait," Hugh replied.

"Most bait can't rip off the fish's head."

"It does not matter. No one came to see," the ghost said.

He almost sounded disappointed. Shane trusted him less now than he had before, which hadn't been much. But he still wanted the ghost's help to find the boats, so he would bite his tongue and say nothing.

"Sure. So can you keep going, or is this really as far as you can go?"

"I might go a little farther yet," the ghost said.

Shane laughed again.

"Of course you can."

CHAPTER 21
DARK TERRITORY

Shane and Hugh continued north. The ghost had little explanation for his test other than hoping to capture some of the other cannibal spirits in a trap. Shane wasn't sure if he bought it. Not that he thought Hugh was trying to kill him. If that was his goal, it was a grossly inefficient way to pull it off.

"What will you do if we clear this island? Of people, the other ghosts, everything," Shane asked.

"What do you mean?"

"What's your plan? That's what you want, right? For the others to be gone?"

"I will do nothing," Hugh said.

"Just sit in the woods until the end of time?"

"I will do nothing," he said again.

His tone was flat and emotionless. He didn't feel sorry for himself, and he wasn't angry. It sounded like he genuinely meant it. He planned to do nothing. As a ghost, he didn't need to do anything. He could stay in one place forever, or as close to it as any ghost was likely to get.

Shane wasn't sure he had met a spirit with no motivation. Many in Hugh's position would want to leave the island. Maybe return to wherever they came from or even be destroyed. Shane had ended more than one ghost that felt like it had outlived its purpose, doing it as a favor rather than something that needed to be done to an enemy.

He wasn't going to tell Hugh that he was making a bad choice or that he could have done all kinds of things. Shane didn't care that much. He was curious, though. It was interesting to see what was motivating the ghost. There seemed to be absolutely nothing. Whatever got the job done, Shane supposed.

They passed beyond the dry, skeletal-looking trees that had been adorned with corpses and returned to open land on the eastern edge of the dwindling maple forest. The elevation at this end of the island was considerably greater than where the village was. The cliff that led to the ocean was quite high. Falling off would have certainly killed anyone, if not by being dashed on the rocks, then by being caught in the raging surf that crashed against the wall below.

Perhaps the tree growth was so limited because of the elevation. The winds were stronger, and the few trees that dotted the landscape were often small and bent. They were fewer and farther between, and Shane saw ahead that they eventually petered off almost completely, with just a random one or two spotting the landscape at odd intervals.

Shane was not sure how much farther Hugh could go, or if the ghost had even been telling the truth. They had to be getting close to a mile from the village. If he was bound to it, his range would come to an end anytime.

"Look," Hugh said as they continued their walk.

The ghost neither stopped nor indicated a direction where Shane was meant to look, or why. Nevertheless, Shane turned his head in time to catch sight of something moving among the sparse trees to the west. He could tell what it was even at a glance: one of the torn-up, cannibalized spirits, scuttling through the snow like a dog.

They continued walking, and he saw a second, and then a third. Shane assumed that the fourth was among them as well, but they were not traveling as a single unit, so it would be easy to mistake one for another at the distance they were at. The group was pacing Shane and Hugh to the north.

"Once we can no longer travel together, they will surely attack," Hugh said.

"This another test?" Shane asked.

"No. This will be an attempt to kill and devour you."

"And if we stay together?"

"Then you will never get to the north edge of the island, and this walk will have served no purpose other than to waste time and put more lives at risk."

Shane nodded. The ghost had a way with words. He stopped walking, and Hugh stopped with him. The ghosts in the woods stopped as well. Shane saw them behind small snowbanks and tree trunks, but none ventured closer. They were waiting for him to make a move.

He suspected that Hugh was right and that they were doing it on purpose. They knew the two would have to part ways, and that would make Shane an easier target. Like separating a weak member from the pack.

Shane could confront them where they were, and attack them in the woods, but he suspected they would have run. He didn't think they would be willing to engage with both Shane and Hugh if they didn't have to. And they knew they didn't have to. He had to keep in mind that even though they looked like animals, they were smart. Devious and crafty.

Hugh was right. If Shane wanted to go north, he had to go north alone. Otherwise, there was no point. In his gut, he did not think that he would find the boats on the northern end of the island. It didn't make sense that Blaine and the others would have taken the boats that far north, docked them somewhere, and then walked back through what Shane just had. There was no way, but he couldn't guarantee it. Maybe he was missing something. And that lingering doubt meant he had to know for sure.

"You might as well wait here. Or go to the east and search," Shane said. "I'll go on alone."

"Are you certain?" Hugh asked.

"Think that's the only way any of this works."

"You are correct. I wish you well, then. If you die, I will tell your friend."

Shane smiled and nodded again.

"I would expect nothing less. Find those boats. I'll be back."

Hugh had nothing else to say. The ghost turned and left, as he had done before. Shane felt that this time he might actually be leaving, not just toying with him. The ghosts in the forest shuffled about, watching the other spirit go back the way they had come. They were probably a little confused at that turn of events, but Shane ignored them and continued onward. They would attack when they wanted to, and he would be as ready for them as he could be.

He saw the northern end of the island on the horizon, and the gray haze beyond that looked like the end of the world, the same one that surrounded the island. Even in the light snowfall, it seemed like there was nothing else in the world but the island. He should have been able to see Canada, he thought, but nothing was out there but snow and rock and waves.

Shane slipped the iron rings back onto his fingers and tucked his gloves into his pockets. He would not be able to take these ghosts on as easily as he had the others. This would require strategy, and he was working on one as the first of them broke free from the trees and came toward him.

They were still not smart with their attacks. They should have attacked as one. That's what he would have done. Instead, only one ran at him, and the others held back as though curious to see what might happen. Maybe they thought that without Frank, Shane would be an easier target this time.

Shane watched as the ghost bounded toward him on all fours. Its skeletal hands dug into the ground, passing through the snow as though it didn't exist. It moved with a wobbly, uneven gait. The lack of muscles covering chunks of its arms and legs made it look like it was learning how to move for the first time. The speed made it bizarre to watch. It was faster than any living man and showed no hesitation.

The ghost skidded to a stop just short of Shane and then circled him quickly. The second and third ghosts were now running at him, and he finally understood the plan. Still, they had waited too long. They put too much time between the first ghost and the others backing it up.

Instead of waiting for all three to join him, Shane dove at the one that had already reached him, catching it by surprise. The ghosts were still not used to anyone fighting them or anyone actively attacking them. They had been looking at the living as food for too long, and not as enemies.

He drove the iron ring into the ghost's temple, and it vanished, thrust back into the forest and wherever its haunted item had been laid to rest. Two others flanked Shane, either as a planned maneuver or a reaction to their companion disappearing. Shane didn't care. He picked the nearest of the two and made a run for it.

The ghost should have backed off and played defensively, but it did not have the wherewithal. When it saw Shane attacking, it turned to meet him. Within seconds, it, too, was sent back to the forest.

Only the third ghost remained, and it was clearly aware that it put itself in a precarious position by attacking, thinking its companions would be there to help it. The ghost paced around Shane. The fourth ghost—the one that had run on two legs at Shane earlier—had not yet shown its face. It had to be nearby, and he did not want to turn his back on anything for too long, in case it was waiting for a chance to strike.

When he moved forward, the ghost moved back. It had learned enough to know not to put itself in harm's way. It was biding its time, waiting for the others to return. Shane was not sure how far into the woods he had sent them, but it would not take long for them to return. There was no sense taking on three at the same time if he didn't have to.

He began to back away, heading north again. The ghost paced him, but if it wanted to stop him, it would have to make a move. Shane was going to force its hand, or it would have to watch him go.

Shane saw the frustration build in the ghost's broken face. Its one eye focused on him intently and, after he had traveled several yards away from their initial meeting place, it moved faster, rushing at him as though intimidating him into stopping. It circled and got in front of him again, but Shane did not slow down. He pressed forward, and it ducked away. This time, he gave chase.

Though it scrambled, Shane bolted after it, catching it off-guard. He reached out with one hand and grabbed the ghost's ankle. That was all it took for the iron ring to have its effect. In an instant, Shane was face-down in the snow alone. The ghost was gone.

There was no way to know where the haunted items for the ghosts were in the woods. He didn't think they were buried under the gravestones at which they consumed most of their victims, but they might have been nearby. They had to feel safe there like it was their home turf. If that was the case, there was a reasonable distance between there and where Shane was. It also meant that he might be able to reach a point where they could not follow.

Hugh was rooted to the village, but the space between the village and the ring of stones in the woods was not that large. He was not sure how far it was to the edge of the island in the north, but Hugh had mentioned something about that being the Cannibal King's territory, someplace where the others could not follow. If Shane went far enough, they could not chase him. He could handle them on his terms.

Shane ran. It was hard to maneuver in the untouched snow. His feet sank, and each step felt like he was struggling through quicksand. But he kept on, pushing forward.

Minutes passed with no sign of the spirits. He occasionally looked over his shoulder, scanning the dwindling woods for any sign of them, but saw nothing. They might have been sent farther than he expected, or they might have given up. He was not willing to wait them out.

The distant horizon grew clearer, and Shane realized he was closing in on the north end of the island. For a time, he thought he might outrun the ghosts. But only for a time.

Over his shoulder, he caught sight of movement again. Four of them this time, not just three. The fourth must not have joined them before, or perhaps now it intended to rally with them and all four could attack as one.

They came as a group like a hunter with his hounds, one on his hind legs like a man, and the other three like animals. They were closing the gap quickly, not slowed by the snow or cold. Shane had no idea how far he still had to go or how close he was to the edge of their territory, but he did not think he was close enough.

CHAPTER 22

SNOW AND STONE

The ghost that moved like a man outpaced the others. The human body was designed to run on two legs, not four. Even mutilated and not bound by human physics, the other three could not keep pace with the strongest among them.

Shane trudged through the snow as quickly as he could. He needed something to even the playing field; taking on four at once was too much. If they attacked together, there was no way to defend against them.

The trees were few and far between now. It was another snow field like the one that separated the forest from the village. Only this time, on the other side of the field—if Shane got there—was nothing but ocean.

He saw nothing in the distance that indicated there was a way down to the water or any way to find the boats from this end of the island. But it mattered little now whether they were hidden there. He needed to find a place to make a stand without getting killed.

The distance between Shane and the ghost shrank. It was moving faster than he could hope to keep up with. He struggled toward an invisible line, some border that might not have even existed, but he knew that soon enough, he would have to give up that fight and take the ghost on.

Shane did not like to run from a fight, but he was not stupid enough to get himself killed for his pride. He fought on his terms, not on those decided by things that were barely human. He just needed to find their limitations, and how far they could travel. But time had run out.

The ghost had caught up with him. Shane knew it was coming, he kept running and waiting for it, and when it was close enough, he ducked into a roll through the snow. It slowed his momentum quickly with minimal impact. The ghost lunged for him and missed, grossly misjudging where he would be, thanks to the effect of the snow dragging him to a stop.

Both recovered quickly. Shane got to his feet, and the ghost squared off with him, looking like it wanted to spar. It stayed on two legs, its arms extended as though they were about to begin a wrestling match, and they circled each other until Shane's back was to the north.

The other ghosts approached quickly, and Shane only had seconds to do something. He kept his back to the north and backed up slowly. He kept his eyes on the ghost, glancing occasionally at the others.

The ghost growled at him, a noise deep in its throat that sounded wet and loose like someone producing phlegm. The exposed muscles around its jaw tensed and flexed, and the few muscles it had across its chest and arms seemed to vibrate.

One of the running ghosts came to an abrupt halt. It stopped like it had been dragged to the ground some twenty yards from where Shane stood. He had seen the effect before and recognized it immediately. The ghost had reached its limit. It had traveled one mile from where its haunted item bound it to the earth.

The others were still coming. Their haunted items were not buried together, so the remaining two closed the distance between them. Shane continued to back up, digging his heels into the snow to keep his footing even as he kept his eyes on the upright ghost.

The nearest ghost came at Shane, risking its safety to prevent his escape. It knew what he was doing. It knew he was putting more distance between them so they could not all fight him at the same time. It swung in a wide arc, dragging fleshless fingers through the air like claws where Shane's face had been just a moment earlier.

Shane ducked. He was not fighting, he was evading. Instead of aiming for a vital spot or even a crippling blow, he gave the ghost a quick backhand slap across the forearm. The iron ring hit bone, and the ghost vanished.

With the nearest threat eliminated, Shane turned quickly, using his hands to dig into the snow and running on all fours briefly until he could get upright and keep moving. The others pursued, and soon enough, another faltered. The third was closing in, with only a few yards separating them. Shane heard it chatter its teeth, clacking like rocks being banged together, and then it suddenly gave a stifled cry, the sound of frustration.

Shane turned and saw that the third ghost had reached its limit. All three were now stuck in place, staggered in a line behind him, held back by an invisible leash. They gnashed their teeth, clawing at the snow, and kept fighting against the bonds that held them. They moved forward inches and then rocked back like a hand was pushing them back to where they had started. The force of the connection to their haunted item was unbreakable.

The fourth ghost appeared again. He was sprinting with ferocity as Shane backed off. He put several yards of distance between himself and his would-be attacker and then watched as this ghost came up short, too. The group had waited too long to attack. They should have tried their luck when he was still with Hugh, and now, none of them could reach him.

The trees had run out. There was no forest anymore, just a handful of maple, poplar, and ash trees scattered about haphazardly in a mostly empty field. The ocean waited in the distance to the north. That was Shane's goal, the place he needed to go. Where everyone was expecting him to go. But he was not ready yet.

He watched the fourth ghost, just a few yards ahead of the third, pacing. It flexed its fingers and gnashed its teeth like a caged animal in a zoo. If it could get free, it would kill. If the ghost had just a few more yards, it would kill. Or it would try, at least.

"Too slow, huh?" Shane said.

The ghost stared at him. Half of the flesh on its face had been chewed away. Someone had eaten its nose and one of its eyes. But there was enough face left for it to look angry. Shane imagined it didn't have many other expressions.

"This all you do? Run? Eat? Look pissed off?"

The ghost's teeth clacked. Shane hoped something would get through. Hoping that, as bestial as these ghosts were, they were still men inside somewhere. But the more he talked, the less the ghost seemed to understand. There was nothing in the one good eye that indicated it heard or understood him.

"There's a light on but no one's home, huh?" Shane said.

Only rage from the ghost. There was no spark behind that eye. Shane didn't think the others would be any different. Hugh had gotten off easy. He had retained who he was, mostly. These things had lost their humanity. The things nailed to the trees had even lost their spirit.

Shane wasn't sure if he pitied these ghosts. They didn't deserve pity. They reminded him in some ways of the Dark Ones in the basement of his home. They had endured torture and had been murdered in the most brutal way, but they chose to become monsters. They didn't have to be that way. Even if these things couldn't think like men anymore, not all animals were bloodthirsty.

Instead, he looked at them the same way he might look at a rabid dog. They needed to be put down. For their good and the good of everyone that might come across them. The four, and the Cannibal King most of all.

The four of them were staggered. Shane could take them out one at a time, and they would not be able to help one another. Maybe the others would flee if he took out the one in front. Maybe they would realize what he was doing and run to a place where they could be together and fight together. But he could destroy this one. The one that still stood upright like a man.

Shane took a step forward. Just one.

Ahead of him, to the south, the deep, loud bellow of the Cannibal

King resonated through the forest. It was closer than Shane had ever heard it. So close that he was surprised he did not see the ghost. The others forgot about him as though he didn't exist.

The ghost that ran like a man bolted the moment the sound pierced the still air of the island. The other three waited for him and then joined him as they ran on all fours at his side. They vanished in moments, back into the forest from which they came. Shane didn't know if they were going after the other ghost or fleeing it. Neither mattered to him at that moment. He was free again. He could head to the north ledge, look out, and see if the boats had been left somewhere. Finally learn if there was a way to get off the godforsaken island.

He headed north, pushing his way through deeper and deeper snow. The wind had carried it up toward the northern edge. Now that there were no trees in the way to cut back on the accumulation, the drifts were larger. His progress slowed considerably, and he checked over his shoulder regularly. There was no sign of his four pursuers, nor the ghost they feared. It was as though Shane had become irrelevant.

The sound of the waves grew louder, and the wind was stronger and colder coming off the sea. The rocky edge of the island was jagged and irregular, jutting up and down like someone had smashed rocks out of the way and left the remains behind to serve as a border to the field of the forest within.

Shane headed to the farthest point he could see, right to the edge of the island. He stood on the rocks and looked at the sea below. As far as he could see in either direction, there were only crashing waves on stone. There was nowhere that a boat could have landed and nothing even close to a beach. The sheer face of the rock went straight down to the water. No one had taken the boats to the north.

There could have been a cove or maybe a small inlet, but how would anyone have gotten back to the island? How would Blaine have managed it? There were no trails or ladders. The north was the dead-end Shane feared it would be. He had wasted his time.

Shane turned and looked back the way he had come. He could follow the eastern wall as far as he had gone alone and see if there was anything he had missed on his way up or anything Hugh had not found, but he had little faith.

He hoped Frank had better luck.

CHAPTER 23
THE SHADOW

Shane had returned to the trees that had once housed the dead. There were no bodies hung up on branches, and everything was as he left it. The ghost of Hugh Carson was also nowhere to be seen.

The ghost was still likely checking the shoreline. There was a lot to cover if he headed from the north all the way south along the eastern wall. Shane wanted to believe that the boats were there somewhere, and he thought it was more likely they would be closer to the village than farther. The fact that no one on the island had any idea where the boats might go was a testament to the lack of curiosity that everyone seemed to have. They accepted that things on the island were to be a certain way, up to and including death.

Shane resolved to head back to the village and check in with Frank. Hugh would get back to them when he learned something, but Frank might have discovered a simpler answer in town. If he convinced more people to get on their side and understand the stakes, someone would likely know where Blaine and his two dead friends had docked the boats. If push came to shove, Hugh could just circle the island and find out where they were.

Shane made his way through the trees that once held the corpses, and his eyes drifted again to the maple forest on his right.

There was movement in the trees. It was not the four ghosts that had run off, though. At first, he thought it might be Hugh, but as he walked, the figure in the woods paced him, and he could see that it was not Hugh.

Shane was being followed by a shadow of immense proportions.

There was a significant distance between them, and it walked among the trees, which made it hard to see clearly. But based on Shane's estimate, the shadow was of a man nearly seven feet tall. It was not below a ghost to appear differently than it normally would, casting illusions and making the unreal seem real, but Shane did not get that feeling about this ghost.

He was looking at the Cannibal King, and the ghost wanted him to know. He matched Shane's pace and made no effort to hide. He wanted Shane to know he was there.

The ghost was broad, and he had a shaggy mane of hair atop his head. Shane could not see clearly—the spirit was just a silhouette in the trees—but his body looked lithe. If the story Shane had heard was true, the man it was would have starved to death after eating the remains of everyone else on the island. He would have grown thin, wizened, and weak as his body broke down.

From his size, Shane guessed that his crash would have come quickly. With no food to sustain a man of that size, he would have grown weak. His body would have turned inward, and he would have quickly lost fat and muscle tissue. By the time he died, he would have looked ragged and sallow.

The ghost stopped, and Shane stopped as well. He watched the ghost turn to face him. Even though he could not see the spirit, he knew it was looking at him. Shane's eyes took in the shape of the thing, the size of him, and he noticed that the hair that framed his head was split by two shapes on either side. Something protruded from the skull in silhouette, and it looked to Shane like antlers.

It was not the first time Shane had seen a ghost alter its appearance, but this one was unique. The antlers looked like those of a stag, eight points that he could count on each side.

There was a moment when the world seemed to fall still. The gentle breeze, the slow falling flakes of snow, and even the crashing waves of the ocean faded away. There was only Shane and the shadow staring at each other across fields of snow and trees.

The shadow raised one hand, clenched into a fist, above its head. It looked like a salute, a rallying call, or a signal of triumph. The bellow Shane had heard several times sounded again. This time, it was almost deafening.

Shane almost flinched; the sound assailed his ears so sharply and so suddenly that it was a surprise. He felt it in his teeth, rattling the bones of his jaw, and his skull. The vibration settled into his guts, and the sound was like a thousand lions roaring as one.

The ghost had mastered illusion in a way that Shane had not seen. It used physical manifestations and feelings that he could not escape or see through. They were effective, and against normal people—like the many victims who must have fallen to him in the past—they would have been terrifying.

Wind rose from the east, rising up Shane's back and chilling him through his coat. It was as though a switch had been flipped, and the slow, fat, lazy flakes that fell gently from the sky were wiped clear from the atmosphere and replaced with a violent flurry.

The island howled and the winds raced through the caverns below the ground, creating the desperate moan Shane remembered from the last blizzard. The wind tore at him, buffeting him from behind so forcefully that it almost pushed him forward. He turned his head and saw thick, black clouds rolling in off the ocean.

The storm had come from nowhere; the horizon had been clear only minutes earlier. The ghost was bringing on the weather with a fury. There was no storm building, there was simply a storm. It was as though it had been dropped on the island, slammed down like a hammer hitting a nail.

Cold air battered Shane, froze his face with a biting insistence, and made him pull his hat down toward his eyes. He tried to keep the shadow where he could see it, so it could not surprise him, but it was gone the moment the storm hit.

Shane turned, looking in all directions. He saw nothing but snow, falling fast and thick, whiting out the world around him. The ocean was barely visible to his left, and the forest was all but obscured to the right.

Fighting ghosts in those conditions would put him at a serious disadvantage. He did not want his first meeting with the Cannibal King to be on the ghost's terms in the middle of a blizzard.

He started back toward the village. It was a smart play. The only one, really. He couldn't be caught out in the storm like the one the ghost had brought in. No one would survive long in such fierce, freezing winds.

The blowing snow made the path ahead of him into a kaleidoscope of monotone. White, gray, silver, and shadow wove together, over and over, showing nothing but teasing so much. Sometimes, it looked like the world was unfinished, and other times, Shane thought he saw trees or figures coming toward him from the haze.

The same happened to his right throughout the maple forest that he knew was to the west but was now barely visible. He caught glimpses of darkness there, glimpses of what must have been the Cannibal King, but he weaved in and out of view, sometimes even as Shane focused on him. The spirit would appear, disappear, and then reappear.

Shane thought the ghost might attack, but it became clear soon enough that it had no intention of doing that. He was taunting Shane, walking at his side, as it were. He wasn't in a rush, he got no closer, and he did nothing threatening.

The ghost was keeping his distance. The game he played was more of a pissing contest, Shane guessed. He was showing off, showing Shane what he could do. It was like somebody in a gunfight throwing down their weapons and offering to fight with their bare hands. The ghost was trying to intimidate Shane. Maybe even humiliate him.

Perhaps he had seen Shane fight the other spirits. He must have known that Shane could fight, could pose a threat to him that others couldn't. But he was showing off how little he cared. In essence, he was suggesting that he could kill Shane without touching him. That's what Shane thought, anyway.

Shane's progress was slow. The wind seemed to come straight at him no matter what direction he faced. The snow fell in massive clumps, and the buildup on the ground was coming so fast that he could almost see the levels rise. His tracks from earlier were already halfway filled in, and the storm had barely raged for more than a few minutes.

Shane watched the antlered shadow as it followed through the trees, fading in and out of view. He wondered if the ghost would follow him to the village. He couldn't let it trail him to the town and then start killing people.

He didn't want to fight the ghost in the blizzard, but if he gave Shane no choice, that was what he would do. Shane's plan was to head to the field, the empty space between the forest and the village. If the ghost insisted on coming with him and following as though everything was happening at his leisure, Shane would put him in his place at that time. Whatever it took.

Sometimes, the shadow vanished for minutes at a time, but Shane covered little ground during his absences. The storm was directed right at him, and even when he walked at an angle, the wind turned to compensate. He quickly abandoned the plan, realizing it would only cost him more time if he zigzagged his way back, and focused on heading straight into it.

When Shane was about halfway back to the village, the ghost appeared in different places. It was on his left now, waiting at the farthest edge of the island, just before the rocks that gave way to the ocean below.

The ghost was much closer, but he was still nothing but a shadow and darkness like those things that resided in the basement of the house on Berkley Street. Just dark and horrible, the antlers rising high above his head, proud and clear. It looked like a crown, Shane thought. Intentional, no doubt. Cannibal King. The thing that even the dead feared.

Sometimes, the King was in the trees to the west; sometimes, he waited ahead as though he had stopped and waited for Shane to catch up. He never got close enough to attack or for Shane to see his face. Shane only saw the tall, menacing shape of a thin, wiry man with hair like a wild animal's.

Shane wondered where the four ghosts were, the victims of the King who had fled when they heard his cry in the north. Hugh made it seem like they were the King's jailers, but perhaps their low numbers had thrown off the balance so badly that they had abandoned even trying. Perhaps now they wanted nothing to do with the larger ghost, and they would let him have his way in the village. They would let him kill the living people and deprive themselves of their imaginary food source.

The wind continued to wail, moaning through the unseen caverns in the rock. The moans were like those of the dying. They were mournful, even painful, and they sounded nearby. Shane turned more than once, thinking something was at his side, and saw only the swirling snow.

Other sounds came above the wind through the storm. They fought against the harrowing echoes that came from the rocks below and the blasting wind from the clouds above. They were sounds from the forest, things that Shane had never heard. They sounded like voices and cries, but they were different from the howling wind. These were not distortions or natural phenomena. What he heard sounded like people in pain.

The King's shadow was missing again as Shane forged through snow that was nearly knee-deep in some areas. A shape appeared on the horizon, one that didn't vanish in the swirling snow, and it became clear that he was seeing a tree as he got closer.

The tree was tall, devoid of branches for the first ten feet of the trunk. When he got closer, he could see that there had been branches, but they were broken off. One of them jutted out sharply, and a body hung on it. It was fleshless and dry, little more than a husk. Shane stared at the figure. More trees awaited him beyond this one. He saw other shapes attached and other bodies strung up.

He looked to his right. The forest was gone, but the sound of the ocean was there. To his left, the fading and intermittent images of maple trees dotted the landscape in the storm.

Shane cursed. He was traveling north again. The ghost had spun him around, made him backtrack a considerable distance in the same way he and Frank had wound up in the northeast earlier. And the dead, the things attached to the trees, had returned.

CHAPTER 24
LOST IN NOTHINGNESS

Shane turned to the right and started walking through the snow toward the sound of the ocean. The shift had been instantaneous. He was traveling north now when he was certain the ocean had been on his left only moments earlier. But he had lost considerable distance. He couldn't allow the ghost to do that to him again.

He wondered if the King planned to attack him. He seemed like he was just going to wait Shane out. The spirit could freeze him to death, nail him to one of those trees, eat the flesh from his bones, or whatever he wanted.

The illusions that the ghost cast were complex, very different from the ones Shane was used to. He usually saw through tricks, found the ghosts where they were hiding, and dealt with them. But the King could merge the reality of the island with his illusions. The storm was real, but how real, Shane couldn't say. The ghost could manipulate the weather, change it, and make it seem worse than it was. It also made Shane lose track of which direction he faced and go the wrong way.

So saturated was the land with the ghosts and their essence that it was like Shane's home in Nashua. The house could change, it could alter its hallways and make rooms appear and disappear. Somehow, that same ability had taken root on Maple Grove Island. But instead of walls and hallways, it was the trees and the land. Either the dead controlled it, or the land had absorbed some malevolent intent from them that it could use it against the living.

Maybe it was not the King. Maybe the island, the trees, and even the sky above were all part of the same force. The same haunted presence that mirrored the house on Berkley Street but more intensely. The island had likely been haunted far longer than the house had. Maybe the King had learned how to use it to his advantage.

Shane reached the eastern edge of the island. He saw the gray ocean below, a smudge of movement beneath the blizzard that separated them. The waves crashed, and the sound echoed up to his ears against the rocks. He started south again, sticking close to the wall. The ghost, the island, whatever was doing it could not turn him around so easily again with a landmark nearby. As long as he kept the wall to his left, he would eventually reach his goal.

His path put him at more risk. The raging wind could turn at any moment, and one bad step in the snow could send him tumbling to his death. The ghost could confront him finally, too. Either the four or the King could take advantage of his position. It would be easy enough for one of them to sacrifice themselves by tackling him. They would survive, and he would not.

The snow was not as deep along the eastern edge of the island, and that allowed him to gain some speed again and make up some ground. With the raging blizzard around him, there was little to see or focus on besides putting one foot in front of the other. He kept watching the land, looking for any sign of the King or the other spirits, but nothing appeared.

Shane did not think the King was done with him. He must have been planning something else or just waiting to see what happened. It was just as well that the ghost was biding his time. Shane needed to make up ground, and he didn't want to waste any more effort on wondering what the ghost was up to.

He had walked for nearly half an hour when he saw a shape taking form on the horizon. He could have been at the sugar shack by now. It was hard to gauge how far he had come or how fast he traveled. With nothing to look at for a landmark, and the struggle through the snow causing him to speed up and slow down at irregular intervals, he was having trouble mapping his progress. That the ghost had turned him around once didn't help much, either.

Shadows played before Shane's eyes and then, soon enough, what he saw became clear. Not the shack where he had left Lonnie and the other men. It was a group of trees. All of them were covered in peeling, papery bark, and the lower branches cut away. Bodies were thrust upon the higher ones.

Shane had turned his eyes for a fraction of a second to focus on the trees in front of him. In that time, he had been moved. He was no longer standing next to the ocean. The rock wall did not fall away in the treacherous cliffs on his left. Instead, the forest was in the distance. To his right, many yards away now, was the ocean. He was facing north again. He was back at the same place that he had fought the slow ghosts.

Shane held back some choice swear words and instead readjusted his gloves and coat, taking a moment to focus on something else to calm his rising anger. He wanted to find the ghost and break his arms, tear the antlers from his head, and shove one down his throat. But the ghost was hoping Shane would make a mistake, lose his focus, or give up. Shane wouldn't let him win so easily.

The island—or the ghost—did not want Shane to return to the village. And if he did not return to the village, he would die. So, whatever was happening was designed to kill him. That was the simple, easy conclusion.

Shane changed direction again. Not south, or what he expected to be south, and not east. He headed for the woods this time. The forest of maple trees was his destination. The home of the Cannibal King and whatever power was working against him.

Shane did not understand how the house on Berkley Street worked. He did not know if it could think or if it was a living thing with conscious desires. If the woods were the same way, they would push him as much as they could but would likely not be able to kill him. They would lead him to his death in other ways: freezing, falling to the ocean, running into the King… Shane decided to help it along. He would head into the belly of the beast and see what happened.

The wind raged and came down into his face, freezing the exposed flesh. It pushed at him, tugged at his clothes, and winnowed its way into all the open cracks and crevices so that his body was soon chilled. Still, he pushed forward.

The trees appeared and disappeared in the swirling blizzard, and for one instant, he thought he saw the King there, antlers atop his head, neck crooked slightly as if confused by Shane's course of action. But the swirling snow was too fast and too blinding, and the shape vanished as quickly as it had appeared.

Shane reached the cover of the trees, but they provided little relief from the storm. The snow was not falling in any one direction any longer; it circled him.

He headed deeper into the woods. The snow was not as deep as it had been, and the trees had broken up the accumulation enough that there were peaks and valleys, making it easier to walk sometimes and more difficult at others. He had learned his first time through the woods that it was easy enough to follow the valleys, to stride from one to another and make progress, even if his path was not straight or simple.

Shane saw the King more clearly from within the trees. The shape, shadowy and still hiding his true face, was easier to track with the trees blocking some of the snow. When Shane moved, it moved as well, striding easily from maple to maple, keeping out of sight except for when he wanted to be seen.

The ghost traveled deeper into the woods, and it was easy enough for Shane to guess that the spirit was leading him somewhere. Luring him into a trap, most likely, or tricking him again by disorienting him.

Shane felt the arrogance coming off the spirit. The King was supremely confident. He was mocking and teasing Shane, but he was still focused. His apparent lack of caring was exposed as nothing more than a performance given how much he cared, and how often he appeared just beyond Shane's field of vision, to draw him in more and more. Even though the ghost wasn't fighting or engaging Shane, he did not want Shane to leave.

Have it your way, Shane thought. He was happy to let the ghost continue and happy to let him think he was in charge. All he needed to do was get close enough. To let the ghost think that he was going to take Shane on, kill him, eat him, or whatever his plans were. All Shane had to do was get within arm's length. One touch of an iron ring and the King would be sent back to whatever ramshackle castle he came from.

He hoped that banishing the King would put a damper on the storm or cut it back some. It started with a signal from the ghost, with his fist raised in the air, so even if it was the will of the island doing it, the ghost was still involved. Without his presence, it might die down or become easier to manage. And then Shane could head south again. Maybe in time to make it to the field beyond the woods.

He picked up the pace, following the ghost and closing the gap between them. He knew that the King was aware of what he was doing, but the spirit continued as if everything was the same. He did not increase his speed to match Shane's or try to get away.

Shane was wary that the ghost had a plan, and it was obviously anticipating the moment when they crossed paths. It was easier to deal with a trap that you were walking into if you knew you were walking into it. Shane would just have to be faster.

He closed in on the ghost until only a few trees separated them. Then something snagged Shane's ankle. He thought briefly it was a root, an errant branch on the ground, but then it closed around his leg and pulled back violently.

Shane fell face-first into the snow. He tried to roll but something was on him in an instant. Cold, clammy fingers wrapped around his face and covered his mouth as he was dragged behind a tree and propped up, facing out into the blizzard at nothing while the ghost held him from behind.

"Stop," Hugh said in his ear just as he began to fight.

Shane was breathing heavily, and the smell of the ghost was like rotten meat and old motor oil. He resisted the urge to struggle and his instinct to tear the ghost's hand from his wrist and then break off the arm. Hugh was not fighting him or doing anything else. The ghost was simply holding him with a hand over his mouth.

"You need to leave now," the ghost whispered.

His hand slipped free from Shane's mouth, but he was still holding him, his back against a tree as he held Shane from behind.

Shane was on his backside in the snow as his breathing slowed. He pushed Hugh's hand away and moved, putting distance between them so he could turn and face the spirit, sitting in his froglike crouch.

"What the hell are you doing?" Shane whispered.

"You were about to die, and it was not going to be a quick death. It would be long, and painful, and you would pray for the storm to freeze you so that it would stop."

"You're very presumptuous," Shane told him.

"I have been here longer than you. I don't need to presume."

"You don't know—" Shane began.

"No." Hugh cut him off. "*You* don't know. The Wendigo was not stalking you for fun. He is learning. He has not been this far south in so long. He's getting the lay of the land. He's hunting. You, the others, the villagers. He knows there are no longer enough of the others to keep him in check. Do you understand what this means? He knows he's free. This storm is his reckoning. He is coming for everyone, and if he had gotten you, if you were the first, he would have made you suffer in ways you could never imagine."

CHAPTER 25
THE COLD HAND OF DEATH

"Then we should take him on now. Here. While he thinks he has the upper hand. He's never fought you or me. He's overconfident," Shane said.

The King was nowhere to be seen, but the storm still raged. Shane crouched across from Hugh, hidden in a small circle of trees while the wind howled and raged.

"Overconfidence is in abundance," Hugh told him. "I have not fought him because I don't want to. He would destroy me. And he would destroy you. I will not spare your feelings or keep you out of harm's way. I have no loyalty to you. But you can destroy the others, and I would rather you stayed alive to do that and then get the people off this island. Make it so he has no one left to kill. Render him as good as dead."

"If you've never challenged him, you don't know," Shane said.

"Have you ever challenged a lion? A bear?" Hugh countered. "I have seen him fight. I have felt how he kills. He is not like the others. He is not like anything I have ever seen."

Shane did not like the way Hugh did things, but he would be a fool to ignore the ghost's words. He knew better than Shane did, and he had much more experience. Even if he seemed overly cautious, Shane had to defer to him. And he had to admit, the Cannibal King was not like other ghosts he'd encountered, either. The way he controlled illusions, and the way he presented himself—even the physical size—was unique.

It was the opportunity that Shane hated to pass up. He knew the ghost was overconfident, but maybe Shane was falling into the same trap. As much as he didn't want to admit it, it was smarter to err on the side of caution.

Shane didn't much like Hugh. He didn't care for the way the ghost conducted his business. He didn't like his attitude and his unpredictability. He also didn't like the way he seemed disinterested enough to just watch Shane die if the opportunity arose. But he knew more than Shane did. Shane had to accept that and take it for what it was worth.

If Hugh had wanted to harm him, he would have done so by now. Even if Shane didn't agree with his methods, the ghost was helping. Maybe his help was not the kind that Shane thought everyone needed, but he was still willing to extend some trust toward him.

"I need to do something," Shane said.

"You can," Hugh replied. "When the Wendigo came for you, the others fled. They knew that both of you were in the north, so they went south. They've been circling the village. They will kill those people soon if they haven't yet. That's why I came to get you."

Shane stared at the ghost in disbelief.

"You could have led with that." He growled and got to his feet.

The ghost rose easily to a standing position as Shane trudged southward through the snow.

"I would have, but you were intent on killing yourself."

The storm was still pummeling the island, but the King had vanished. Shane looked for him, watching the forest intently as they traveled, until Hugh intervened.

"He is gone. I hid you from him. He probably thinks one of the others killed you. He didn't care enough to check. That is how little he thinks of you," the ghost explained.

"Good to know. I'll be happy to change his opinion when I get the chance."

"So you seem to think," Hugh replied.

Whatever illusion that had Shane walking in circles had lost its hold. Either because the King had left, or because Hugh had intervened, they were eventually able to leave the forest. Soon enough, the tree cover gave way to the open field.

It was impossible to see the village, smoke from the little chimneys, or anything else. The whiteout of the blizzard had only gotten worse, and it played havoc with Shane's eyes. It was hard to tell whether he was seeing ten feet or ten yards in front of him. Everything was obscured in the storm.

They crossed the field in silence. The howling of the wind vibrated through the ground and into Shane's legs, rumbling in the caverns under the island. Hugh traveled by his side, his legs passing easily through the snow, unaffected by the physical world. He kept pace with Shane, didn't rush, didn't say anything, and kept his eyes forward.

Shane looked back on occasion, but the forest was gone in moments, and any chance of seeing the four spirits or the King vanished with it. Even still, he didn't get the sense that they were being followed or watched. Hugh had been right: The King didn't care enough about him to bother.

They reached the edge of the village, the bowl that led into the depression where all the little cabins waited. The southern end of the village was still obscured, but Shane saw several closer buildings in the flurries of snow. No one was outside, but he didn't expect them to be in the storm. Drifts built along the sides of all the cabins, nearly up to the windows in some cases. But no smoke came from the chimneys.

"There." Hugh pointed into the storm.

Shane squinted against the blowing of the wind. There might have been something farther into the village. Maybe smoke, quickly being pulled away from a building, but the gray on white was too hard to see. It looked like the Great Hall, though. That would make sense. Especially in the storm, people would need to stay warm and eat meals, and it was a good place to spend time with others. Frank would have gathered people, and it was the only building suited to the task.

They descended the edge of the bowl into the town. Shane wondered whether Frank had made progress on finding the boats. Even if they had discovered them, the storm made it impossible to leave the island. They would need to wait it out. To hear Hugh tell it, that would be impossible. Shane would have to prove the ghost wrong.

The snowy pathways were even harder to traverse in the village. The bowl, which usually protected the village, now acted as a focal point for the blizzard. The snow gathered there. The whole place would be snowed in soon enough if the storm did not subside. As it was, it was more than knee-deep as Shane worked through it.

He saw no lights on in any of the cabins by the outskirts of Maple Grove. But as the Great Hall came into view, he saw the flickering glow of the hearth fires within, obscured by the frost-covered windows.

Shane forced his way through the snow, his progress slow and arduous. The flurries swirled around him, very nearly a tornado of snow as it spun and blew in all directions. Something dark caught Shane's attention, pulling his eyes to the nearest of the stone cabins. A shape on the roof was moving, descending not toward him but toward the Great Hall. He recognized it right away.

The ghost was stalking, fixated on the Great Hall and the people inside. It was unaffected by the slippery peak of the roof, navigating with ease as its shredded and chewed arms and legs easily grasped the surface.

"They were here once before but fled. Something must have scared them off," Hugh said, seeing the spirit.

Frank, Shane thought. He could have fought them off. Or at least forced them to leave with the iron rings. But as Shane and Frank already knew, the ghosts were persistent. If all four were there, they would be looking for a weakness, a way to wear Frank down and get past him.

Everyone must have been in the Great Hall. Frank would have herded them together because that was the only hope he had to protect any of them. If anyone had stayed behind in their cabins, they were probably already dead.

A second spirit was already on the ground. It had nearly reached the

Great Hall, heading for the eastern wall of the building. As Shane watched, forcing his legs through the deep, impeding snow, it avoided the door and slipped through the timbers as though they didn't exist.

Muffled screams from within the Great Hall met Shane's ears over the raging sound of the storm.

"Go help," he barked at Hugh.

The ghost did not argue. He ran, passing through the wall of the Great Hall in moments. Shane reached into the snow in front of him as he kept walking, packing together a hasty snowball before throwing it at the roof of the nearby cabin. It passed harmlessly through the ghost, but it got the monster's attention.

"Miss me?" Shane asked.

The ghost stared at him through the blowing snow. This one had no eyes, the empty sockets saw without seeing, and Shane saw the teeth clicking together. He pushed toward the Great Hall, removing his gloves as he trudged near the entrance, and then, he waited.

It did not take long for the ghost to oblige. It jumped from the building and bounded across the snow like it was solid ground. Only four strides separated them, and the ghost lunged at Shane but went low with its attack. Shane thought it had miscalculated at first, and then realized it was going for his legs, beneath the surface of the snow where he could not see or reach it as easily.

Shane stumbled back as the ghost clawed toward him under the snow, sinking ragged, fleshless fingers into his shins. He growled between gritted teeth and fell against the Hall. The ghost pulled its claws free and drew back for a swipe, but Shane was quicker this time.

Pushing off the wall, Shane dove into the snow, catching the ghost's face in his hands. He sunk his thumbs into the empty eye sockets, giving him a grip even as the slimy feeling of the skull resisted being held.

The ghost struggled against him, but it was no use. Shane held it firmly and, when it realized it was at a disadvantage so low to the ground, it rose again. However, Shane had already capitalized on his higher position. He collapsed on his knees in the snow, on top of the spirit, driving it fully into the ground and pulled back with his fingers jammed into its empty eye sockets.

A sound gurgled out of the ghost's half-missing throat, a faint rumbling, as its back arched as much as Shane's knees on its spine would allow. He hooked his fingers deeply into the dead thing's skull and wrenched back with all his might.

The ghost's neck snapped loudly enough for Shane to hear it. Its head hung back loosely in his grip, but he wasn't done. With his fingers from one hand still in its eyes, Shane grasped it by the side of its head and twisted, pulling up at the same time. The ghost's head tore free from its body.

Shane lurched backward with the force of the ghost body blasting apart. It had no effect on the snow or the world around it, but the energy flowed through Shane like a kick to the chest.

His body hit the door to the Great Hall, and it buckled, collapsing inward as he fell to the floor. The warmth of the room washed over him, relieving some of the pain he felt. Dozens of voices screamed and gasped as he tumbled into the room, and in seconds, Clint and Frank were standing over him.

"Are you okay?" Clint grabbed his arm and pulled him up.

"Fine," he replied. "Where's the other one?"

"Gone," Frank flexed his fingers to indicate the iron rings.

Shane pulled away from Clint, giving him a nod, and got to his feet on his own. The entire village looked to have been crowded into the Great Hall. The fires burned brightly as Frank went to the door and closed it, even though the latch was broken after Shane's fall.

"They've been attacking steadily for a half-hour or so," Frank said. "Hugh went to get you. Glad he succeeded."

The ghost stood in the front corner of the hall, away from the living, though everyone could see him. Obviously, Frank had ameliorated their fears and let them know that Hugh was on their side, but the nervous looks in his direction suggested that not everyone was ready to embrace him just yet.

"Well, there's one less now," Shane said.

"Did you find anything?" Frank asked.

"Ghosts," Shane said. "And a hell of a blizzard. The only way we're getting out of here is by destroying these things. Three to go. Then there's the King. How long between attacks?"

Frank could not give an answer, nor did he need to. A scream from the end of the Hall was answer enough. The crowd parted, many running toward the door, and toward Frank and Shane. In the back by the kitchen, one of the ghosts had taken a woman and was climbing the wall, holding on to her with claws embedded in her stomach.

CHAPTER 26

STORM'S END

Shane ran down the table to avoid the cluster of villagers until he reached the far end of the Hall. He was only steps away from the ghost when more screams sounded behind him. The other two had entered the building. Frank put himself between one and Clint while Hugh grabbed hold of the third before it sunk claws into Lonnie.

Shane had no time to worry about the others. He had to focus on the ghost he was closest to and have faith that Frank and Hugh could hold their own.

He reached the end of the table and jumped down. The crowd had parted, putting as much distance between themselves and the ghost as they could. The woman the spirit was dragging through the wall was middle-aged with frizzy brown hair peeking out from beneath a winter cap. She stared at Shane with panicked eyes, screaming for help while the ghost scrambled toward the window so it could take her into the storm.

With one hand full and one pulling itself and the woman up the wall, the ghost had no way to fight back. Shane grabbed it by the leg and pulled hard, dragging it off the wall and the woman with it.

"Go," he yelled at her when she fell in a heap next to him.

To her credit, the woman wasted no time. She bolted, nearly falling again, and ran into the arms of other villagers who pulled her to safety as Shane sunk his fingers into the exposed meat of the ghost's back. He dug in right above its waist and pushed through its ribs. The ghost twisted to roll over so that it was face-up to struggle away, but Shane had a good grip and was scaling its body like he was climbing a wall.

Shane drove his hands into the ghost's midsection, prying bone out of the way and snapping ribs as he worked his way up the slick, squirming body. The ghost bucked and growled, gnashing its teeth and regaining its footing. Shane reached under its exposed rib cage from behind and took hold of its spine, pushing his elbow down on the spirit's neck and then wrenching his arm back violently.

The spine snapped like a piece of dry wood. Its body went limp, no longer writhing and struggling to get away. It was flat on the ground but still gurgling and hissing. Not destroyed, but crippled. Without a functioning spine, it could do nothing.

Shane pulled free and knelt next to the ghost. He held its face flat against the floor of the Great Hall and then slammed his elbow into its skull. Spectral bone shattered and sent a shockwave through his arm as the ghost came apart.

He fell back again, almost hitting the end of the long table, and stared up at the ceiling. The Hall was loud, and voices were talking over one another, screaming and crying.

With a grunt, Shane rolled over and got back to his feet. The ghost that Frank had tangled with was banished again. Hugh was still wrestling with the other one. Now that Shane was finished, the villagers flooded back toward the kitchens, the only end of the building that was free from the spirits.

He passed the woman he had saved, and she reached out for him, grabbing his arm and thanking him. He pulled away with a quick nod. He had no time to worry about what she had to say and ran for Hugh, who was engaged more in a defensive fight than anything else.

After so many years, Shane wondered if Hugh had it in him to destroy something. Not that it would matter if Shane got to it; he just needed Hugh to hold it still for another few seconds.

Despite Shane's intentions, Hugh could not keep hold of the ghost. He wrestled with it and hurled it at the wall. The cannibal spirit's body passed through the door and out into the storm.

Shane followed the ghost outside, throwing open the door, and letting the blizzard back into the building. The spirit darted away, running down the snow-filled street, and Shane gave chase. Hugh and Frank came after him, and the three followed it down the road to the center of town and the stone pillar that waited there.

The ghost reached the pillar and wrapped itself around it as though it thought it might offer it safety. The final spirit was already there, the one that walked on two legs. It stood there as if it had been waiting for Shane to show up, and he met its gaze as he struggled through the snow toward it.

Snow blasted the men from all angles. Shane had no idea where the King was, if he was watching, if he planned to join, or if he had remained in the woods. They could worry about him later. Now, they had only two left. Two to finish and then maybe, finally, they could get the people off the island.

"You can't fight in this," Hugh warned as Shane entered the clearing in the village center.

"Watch me."

He had just about enough of the ghosts of Maple Grove Island. He had decided that the fight would end now, snow or no snow. He would destroy them by himself if he had to.

The spirit that moved like a man ran at Shane. It flew through the snow, not graceful but still swift. It did not use the landscape to its advantage. It wasn't looking to trick Shane or be sly. Instead, it just came at him with arms extended, ready to choke the life from him.

Shane's hands were empty. He wore no rings because he was not looking to send them back to their haunted items. The ghost must have taken that as a sign that he would be easier prey.

They met feet from the stone altar. Shane caught the ghost's arms, digging his fingers into the ragged bits of meat that were still stuck to the bone. This one was harder to grip than the others because there was less to hold on to. The slick bone resisted him, making his hands slide as the ghost reached toward him and fought against him. It went for Shane's throat, to either choke him or tear it from his body and bleed him out right there.

One of the ghost's arms slipped, and claws scraped down into Shane's coat, through the material, and into his flesh.

Hugh intercepted the other ghost before it could join in. He grappled with it next to the altar, his fighting more animated now than it had been in the Hall. Shane kept his focus on the ghost that struggled to reach his neck.

Frank was almost at his side, close but not willing to interfere.

"Fake him," Shane shouted.

Frank was fast. He swung a fist, and the ghost lurched away to avoid the blow that Frank had no true intention of landing. It was enough for Shane to capitalize on. He fell back into the snow and rolled, the bulk keeping him upright enough that it threw the ghost off-balance and forced him to bend but didn't put Shane at a disadvantage.

The ghost's arm twisted, with his hands still caught in Shane's sleeve, and Shane raised a foot. He kicked out, planting his boot in the meatless shoulder. The appendage snapped and tore free. Shane held the arm for an instant longer, and then it faded from existence.

His hands now free, Shane tackled the ghost around the waist. It fell into the snow, and then through the snow, but Shane held onto its head. The body sank out of the way. Shane fell to his knees, held up by the drift under him, and twisted. The ghost's neck broke with a crunch.

Hugh peeled open the second ghost's skull and it exploded, the force pushing Shane back into Frank. He pulled the head he held with him, tearing it from the broken neck, and he and Frank were forced back into the snow as the ghost came apart in a violent rush.

Neither Shane nor Frank moved for a long moment. The blizzard continued to pelt them, covering them with snow where they lay. After a moment, Hugh appeared standing above them, looking down at each man in turn.

"Are you dying?" he asked.

"No," Frank said. "Just taking a moment."

"They have been destroyed. It would be a good time for you to leave."

"Yeah," Shane said. "Give us a few seconds."

The ghost did not reply, he merely stood and waited. Eventually, Shane sat up and Frank joined him. They headed back to the Great Hall, slow and sore.

They had boats to find.

CHAPTER 27

BITTER TEA AND COLD TRUTHS

Shane wrapped a bandage around the cut on his arm. The heat of the fires in the Great Hall slowly warmed him. It felt like days since he had been inside a building or near anything warm. One of the villagers brought him a cup of their bitter, mostly tasteless tea, but he accepted it gracefully, letting the hot liquid burn his tongue at the back of his throat. He didn't care; it was just good to feel something besides cold.

Frank sat across from him at one of the long tables with a cup of tea in his hands. He looked tired, not that Shane blamed him. The wind still howled and raged outside, but the walls of the Great Hall muffled it considerably. Made it feel like it was a dream, something that could be ignored.

"Sir?" One of the villagers approached awkwardly.

Shane didn't recognize the man. He was younger than most of the residents, but not by much. His hairline was receding, and the series of scars on his face looked to be many years old. Shane briefly wondered what attracted him to the island but would never ask.

"Yeah?" he replied.

"I was telling your friend Mr. Benedict earlier that I know where Blaine and the others took the boats. At least I think so."

Shane glanced at Frank, who was listening in.

"Everything happened all crazy before, so I didn't get to talk about it. And honestly, Mallory and Blaine made it sound like you guys were out to get us, so I didn't want to say anything, but—"

"The boats," Shane interrupted. "Where?"

The man looked surprised but then nodded.

"Right. I did a lot of walking around when I first got here, just to clear my head. Down in the southeast, not far from the village, there's a little path through the rocks. It's hard to see unless you're right on it. But if you go down, there's a cove that pushes under the edge of the island. You can't even notice it when you're up top here. It's a natural little marina, and Blaine told me once that they put the boats there sometimes when it gets too rough by the docks. It's the only other place you can leave a boat on the island."

Shane looked at Frank again. They would need the storm to clear up before they checked, but it sounded even closer than the docks. Had the boats been there this whole time? It was frustrating to think of the time they had wasted.

"You think the boats are there now?" Shane asked.

"Like what I said, it's the only other place where you can leave a boat," he replied. "I didn't go and look. But if they're not at the docks, they have to be there."

"We'll look when the storm lets up. Thank you for letting us know," Frank told the man.

"Sure, yeah. I just want to help. This place is not what I thought it was," he replied.

He left them then, heading back to the end of the long table to rejoin the others from the village. Shane took another drink of the bitter tea and met Frank's eyes.

"You think the boats are there?"

"They have to be somewhere," Frank said.

"Do they?" Shane asked.

They had not addressed the possibility that the boats no longer existed. Most of the reason that Hugh, the Cannibal King, and the other spirits were on that island was because they had lost their boats. They'd crashed on the rocks, leaving them stranded. Maybe the boats were supposed to be somewhere but were lost. Maybe they had been sabotaged.

If Shane were one of the ghosts, and he didn't want the people to leave, the first thing he would have done would be to get rid of the boats. Cut off everyone's way to escape. That made sense. If you were looking to trap an animal, you didn't leave it with an easy escape.

"You think they could have been lost?" Frank asked.

"You don't?"

"I had thought of it. I didn't think anyone here would be so stupid, but…"

"Didn't have to be anyone from here," Shane finished.

Frank nodded and sipped his tea.

"Other ghosts are here," Shane told him. "I found some north. Victims of this Wendigo, the Cannibal King. They were weak, though. Slow and frail. When I fought them, it was like they had lost the will to even try. Almost nothing happened when I destroyed them."

"How so?"

"There's usually a massive energy when they go, right? A blast of power like a kick in the gut. But they… just fizzled out."

"Why would something like that happen?" Frank asked.

"Don't know. I think it had to do with how they died. Maybe something that this King does to them. Like he keeps them alive for so long that he saps their will to live. What's left over is more broken than anything I've seen. But they still moved, and they still wanted to kill. If I couldn't fight back, they probably would have overwhelmed me."

"But you handled them," Frank said, not as a question.

"Yeah. But it made me wonder what else is on the island that we don't know about. Hugh was only helping us to get what he wants, and that's everyone gone. He'd happily spend eternity squatting next to a tree doing nothing. He's not motivated to tell us anything that's not related to that goal. He knew about those ghosts, and he watched me fight them. What if there are others? What if someone saw where the boats were left and tore them apart? And now we're stuck here, no boats or radio in a storm that isn't natural."

"Something to think about," Frank agreed grimly.

If the boats were gone, if there were no radios, and if the Cannibal King was controlling the storm with the island, there was one solution. Mo still knew they were there. He might still be looking, just not in weather like that. But if it cleared up, and it was reasonable to get to the island again, he might come back. They needed to make it possible. That meant getting rid of the King.

"No luck finding a radio or a satellite phone?" Shane asked.

"We didn't have much time to put a plan into action to search," Frank said, "but we can do it now."

"That should be our first priority," Shane said. "We can't do anything with boats until the weather clears up, but we can use a radio now."

"If there's anything, we'll find it," Frank said.

The problem was that Shane didn't think they would find anything. He was starting to think that Mallory had been just lost enough in her beliefs to have not left any back doors for herself or her people. It was looking more and more like there was only one solution to their problem. Hugh was going to hate it.

EPILOGUE

The howling wind seemed to come from everywhere at once. Not just the sky above and the ground below, but even the trees themselves. The ghost crawled through the snow, almost hidden in it, save for the top of his head. He had been on the island for a long time. He didn't know how long. It was too hard to keep track of time, and his head felt thick and strange when he tried to remember things from the past.

He remembered his ship scraping across the rocks. He remembered disembarking with his men to investigate the land they had discovered. Even the little village with its stone cabins seemed like a blessing until everyone started to vanish. Wellesley, Morris, Bundy, Carson, and all the others. They all vanished eventually. In the end, he was the only one left. Simon Mackenzie, captain of a forgotten ship. Stranded, alone, and facing death.

He remembered the devils that came for him. Their bodies were chewed and torn almost to pieces. They looked like things that had crawled from the bowels of hell and set their sights upon him. He had tried to run away from them, but he failed.

He begged for mercy when they captured him. He prayed to God. He felt no shame when his screams echoed through the forest as their teeth sank into his flesh and ripped it away in chunks. The pain was not like anything he had experienced or could have ever even imagined.

They had kept him alive for days. His wounds festered, and the sensation of numbness from the cold mixed with the pain to play tricks on his mind. It made no sense that he could feel himself so intensely and also feel almost nothing at the same time. He wished for oblivion.

When death came, it was not peaceful. He did not slip away. It was them, feasting on his remains. Either they no longer wanted to keep him, or their greed became too great. But their teeth were merciless, tearing not just muscle and bone but veins and arteries. He felt himself grow weak as his blood washed through the snow.

His last thoughts were hard to accept because he was so thankful. He was thankful that he was dying, and he never imagined he'd be in such a state. He was relieved that the pain was coming to an end and that he would no longer have to see and endure the horrors. But even that was a lie. Death ended nothing for him, it just started something new.

When he came back and saw the world with fresh eyes, it was somehow the same yet vastly different. Like him, the world was not the way it was supposed to be. He had returned as they'd made him, mangled and ugly. A monster. He was like them now, dead but not gone. Aware and in the world but not part of it. An anguished spirit. He could think of no worse fate. No heaven or hell for Simon Mackenzie, but eternity on the island with the mindless monsters who had feasted upon his flesh.

For years, Simon Mackenzie hid away, keeping his distance from the creatures that made him and the people who sometimes came to the island and fell to the same fate. He hid from the dark thing that lived in the north, and even from the spirit of Carson, which he saw once at a distance but could not bear to face. He could not endure the shame of letting his one-time associate see what had become of him.

Something had recently changed on the island. The storm that raged was not normal; it had never been that bad. The others were gone. Their numbers had dwindled for days. And the thing in the north was coming south. He had seen its shadow.

Something was happening with the people of the island, the ones who lived in the village. Mackenzie had not gotten close enough to learn what they were up to, and a part of him did not want to know. Part of him did not want to be discovered. He was no longer a part of the living world.

What they did didn't matter to him, but he could not help but feel the pull of curiosity now that things were changing after so long.

Mackenzie made his way to the circle of graves in the forest. The stone markers had always attracted the dead, including the things that had killed him. It was the place where they had torn apart his body. He did not know why it was important to them, but it was.

When he got there, he found nothing but snow. White and pure. None of them were there. He wondered if they were all gone now. He wondered what could kill a ghost.

He gave no voice to the thought, but he realized too late that he would get an answer. He was not as alone in that circle as he thought. A shadow moved from the tree behind him. It was not the darkness of the woods or a trick of the storm. The shadow was its own thing, tall and slender. A great rack of antlers rose from its head, piercing the snowy sky above.

Mackenzie moved, but the shadow was much too fast. A hand clutched him, holding him as if he was a real, physical thing again, and lifted him out of the snow.

"What are you?" Mackenzie asked.

The shadowy figure roared, and Mackenzie felt like he was alive again. Not warm or breathing with a heartbeat; he felt the terror he had felt when he was alive. Fear seeped into every ounce of his being as the deafening sound consumed his world, drowned out the storm, and invaded his skull. There was nothing but the shadowy monster and its fearsome cry.

Mackenzie's scream was impossible to hear. He couldn't even hear it in his head as the shadow held him in its large, powerful hands and pulled. He didn't feel it when his body came apart, not the way he used to feel things. But for a moment before there was nothing left, he understood. He had found oblivion.

Check out these best-selling series from our talented authors:

GHOST STORIES

RON RIPLEY

BERKLEY STREET SERIES
MOVING IN SERIES
HAUNTED COLLECTION SERIES
DEATH HUNTER SERIES

IAN FORTEY

JIGSAW OF SOULS SERIES
CULT OF THE ENDLESS NIGHT SERIES

SUPERNATURAL SUSPENSE

A. I. NASSER

SLAUGHTER SERIES
SIN SERIES

DAVID LONGHORN

NIGHTMARE SERIES
ASYLUM SERIES

SARA CLANCY

THE BELL WITCH SERIES
BANSHEE SERIES

For a complete list of our new releases and best-selling horror books, visit ScareStreet.com or scan the QR code below!

www.ingramcontent.com/pod-product-compliance
Lightning Source LLC
Chambersburg PA
CBHW050346030726
47503CB00008B/2638